THE LARK IN THE MORN

Also by Elfrida Vipont

Haverard Family Books

The Lark on the Wing
The Spring of the Year
Flowering Spring
The Pavilion

The Lark
in the Morn

Elfrida Vipont

Illustrated by T.R. Freeman

BETHLEHEM BOOKS • IGNATIUS PRESS
Bathgate   San Francisco

© 1948 Elfrida Vipont

Cover art © 2007 Mary Beth Owens
Cover design by Theodore Schluenderfritz
Back cover decoration by Roseanne Sharpe

First Bethlehem Books Printing September 2007

ISBN 978-1-932350-22-7
Library of Congress Control Number: 2007925231

Bethlehem Books • Ignatius Press
10194 Garfield Street South
Bathgate, North Dakota 58216
www.bethlehembooks.com
1-800-757-6831

Printed in the United States on acid-free paper

United Graphics Inc.
2916 Marshall Ave.
Mattoon, Il 61938
2nd Printing October 2009

Contents

For
Robin, Carolyn, Dorothy
and
Ann

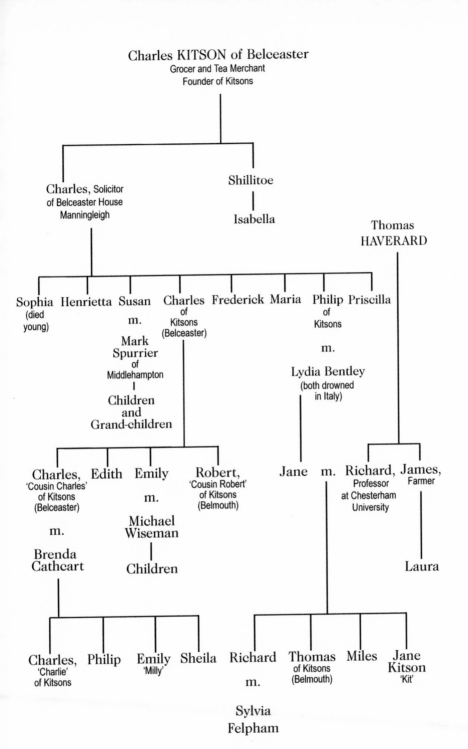

School Terms in This Book

There have been many changes in the English school system since 1948, when this book was written. Many government, or state schools were divided into junior and senior sections: junior from ages 5 to 12 and senior from 12 to 18. In other places there were separate primary and secondary schools. At the beginning of the story, Kit and her friends are at Chesterham High School, a girls' school in the state system. Pony and Helen, who are a little older than Kit, are in the Senior School by Chapter 3. Kit, still in the Junior School, takes the exam for the Junior Medal which will give her a scholarship to pay the fees for the Senior School, and may give her a "double remove," which would mean she would be in the A, or "alpha" stream with Helen, rather than the B or "beta" stream with Pony. Pony is a popular girl, and good at sports, but she is not as clever as Helen.

Later in the story, all three friends have moved to Heryot, a private girls' boarding school run by the Society of Friends, or Quakers. At Heryot Kit takes the School Certificate exam when she is 16, and leaves school after another year. Others stay on to take the Higher School Certificate which qualified one to go to university.

Heryot School is modeled on a Friends' school in York, familiar to the author. "The San," mentioned in some of the later chapters, refers to the Sanitarium, or infirmary.

THE LARK IN THE MORN

As I was a-walking,
* One morning in the spring,*
I met a pretty damsel,
* So sweetly she did sing.*
And as we were a-walking,
* Unto me this did she say:*
There is no life like the ploughboy's,
* All in the month of May.*

The lark in the morn
* She will rise up from her nest,*
And mount up in the air
* With the dew all on her breast.*
And like the pretty ploughboy
* She will whistle and will sing,*
And at night she will return
* To her own nest, back again.*

1. *Over the Wall*

"KIT! KIT! WHERE are you, you impossible child?"

"Here."

"Where?"

"Bedroom."

"What are you doing?"

"Reading."

"Have you done your homework and your practicing?"

"Need I do any moldy practicing? I had a lesson yesterday."

"Of course you must practice, silly! If you're too lazy to do any work, how do you expect your father to go on paying for your music lessons?"

"I don't! I wish he wouldn't!"

"Kit! You ungrateful child! Come downstairs at once and

bring your homework with you."

"I've done everything except the arithmetic."

"Then bring that. Be quick, or you'll not be ready when Pony and Helen come."

Laura Haverard stood in the hall at Thornley Mays, impatiently awaiting her small cousin. The child was always exasperatingly slow. Otherwise she might have been able to help with the spring-cleaning, but as it was, Laura was only too thankful to get her out of the way. Laura herself was very efficient. She prided herself on her orderly methods, but somehow or other she could never instill them into Kit. And if she pressed her too hard, there would only be a tantrum to cope with on top of everything else. Laura hated it when Kit indulged in tantrums. It was such a waste of time. However, if only she could hustle her into finishing her homework, the child would be able to run off and play for the rest of the morning, leaving her free to get on with her work. "For goodness' sake hurry up!" she urged.

Kit came slowly down the stairs with a book under each arm. She looked very untidy, Laura thought. She herself could spring-clean all morning without getting so much as a hair out of place, and her blue overall was as neat as it was becoming. She pulled the child towards her and straightened the collar of her blouse, but what was the use of tidying her up when she never seemed to take any pride in her appearance? She sighed expressively and pushed Kit into the dining-room. "Come along and let's see you start," she said.

Kit sat down at the table and reluctantly opened her books. There were only three sums left. "Measure a room at home and give its area in square feet—"

"You'd better do that now, with my tape-measure,"

suggested Laura helpfully.

"Done it."

"Already? Which room did you measure?"

"Pantry—six feet by four."

"Lazy kid! You don't take a scrap of interest in your work, do you? Now, hurry up, or you'll not be able to go out with Pony and Helen."

Kit wrote "Answer" with a flourish and turned round in her chair. "But we're not going out. It's our Saturday to play here. Don't you remember?"

"No, dear, I don't. And even if it is, you know I can't possibly have you all here today."

"But Laura, we can't change everything now. I do think— it's so jolly unfair—"

"Why don't you go for a nice walk instead?" suggested Laura hurriedly, trying to avert a storm. "It's such a lovely day! You can leave a note for me at Mrs. Campion's, and those books for your father at Joseph Garth Fenwick's."

"Why can't you leave your own silly notes? I don't want—"

"Oh, but you do! And you can play your game, or whatever it is, in the park afterwards. That will be ever so much nicer than being here. Hurry up with that last sum—it's two pounds, fourteen and threepence, if you want to know. I'll let you off your practicing, for once. Run along and ask Martha for some cake."

"All right." Kit shrugged her shoulders as she scribbled down the answer. Arguing with Laura was a waste of time. So were sums. And at least she had got rid of her practicing. She slammed the door as she left the dining-room—"Go back again and shut the door quietly," called Laura from her spring-cleaning—slid along the freshly polished hall and pushed through the green baize door into the kitchen. There was nobody there. The big ginger cat was dozing in front of the fire with his paws tucked cozily in, and tiny motes of dust were dancing sleepily in the broad sunbeams which streamed through the window. The kitchen was a comfy sort of place, thought Kit, much comfier than the drawing-room. It was the only room in the house that had never been changed since her mother's death, so Martha had told her. Even Laura was not allowed to touch it. It was a large, square room, with an old-fashioned range and ample shelves and cupboards: her mother's photograph hung in the place of honor over the dresser. Kit looked at it thoughtfully for a moment, and then sat down on the edge of the spotless deal table, swinging her legs and humming a little tune to herself. Perhaps, after all, it wouldn't be a bad idea to go for a walk. Suddenly the kettle boiled over and Martha came storming in.

Martha Ridyard was a handsome woman, tall, grey-haired and keen-eyed. She had come to Thornley Mays as general servant from the Kitson household at Manningleigh, when Janey Kitson married Professor Haverard. She had always been devoted to Janey. For many years she had ruled the house, not to mention the Professor and his wife, and the three little boys, Richard, Thomas and Miles, who had followed one another in swift succession. When some years later Kit was born, and the children were left motherless, Martha had stood by them staunchly: Janey's children could have had no more faithful guardian. The Professor's niece, Laura Haverard, had come to keep house for him and bring up the family, but one way and another that seemed to make very little difference to Martha.

She entered now in a whirlwind, first to sweep the

kettle off the fire and then to seize upon Kit. "Cake? And what do you want with cake, this time of a morning?" she thundered.

"It's to take out with us. It's our Saturday to play here and Laura won't let us. Isn't she a beast, Martha?"

"Now, don't let me hear you talk like that about Miss Laura. I'll not have it, and well you know it. But it's a shame not to let you play here. You wouldn't be a bit of trouble in the garden. See here, I'll give you each a bit of my bread pudding. I only baked it yesterday."

Martha's bread pudding contained more raisins to the square inch than any of the confections which passed for cake in the dining-room. Kit brightened as she pocketed her trophies. "You're a good sort, Martha," she said. "Sorry I was cross. Hullo, there's Laura calling me. Pony and Helen must have come. Good-bye, and thanks awfully."

Pony and Helen were standing in the hall, talking "company talk." "Oh no, Miss Haverard, we don't mind a bit. It's perfectly all right."

Kit grinned at them secretly as she pulled on her blazer. "Come on, you two. Good-bye, Laura. I'll not be late for dinner."

The front door closed with a bang, and the three ran down to the gate and swung upon it in a meditative row. Pony was the eldest, tall and brown and nearing her teens; Helen the next, bespectacled and clever. Kit, a thin slip of a child, would be twelve in June.

"It's a beastly shame!" she muttered, as they swung to and fro. "But what could I do? Laura's always like that when it's spring-cleaning."

"Let's get the errands done first," suggested Helen, "and then go and play in the fields by the Hall."

"Good for you, Helen," cried Pony, jumping back on to the path. "Come on!"

It was a point of honor with the three never to use the gate, unless compelled to do so by the restraining presence of their elders. Pushing through the murky shrubbery of smutty laurels and rhododendrons, they scrambled on to the parapet of the wall, whence they jumped down, one by one, and so set off, arm in arm, down Thornley Rise, the old main street of Thornley.

There were still elderly people living who referred to Thornley as "the village," but to all intents and purposes it was now part of the great manufacturing city of Chesterham, though some of the features of the old village still lingered. There was the old Hall at the bottom of the main street, with the Home Farm behind, bravely struggling in the soot-laden atmosphere. At the top of the Rise was the old church, and beyond, on the high road to Chesterham, stood the coaching inn, with horse-mount and trough and ample stable-yard, and the weather-beaten sign of the Four-in-Hand creaking in the breeze. Of course the city would win in the end. It was already stretching long covetous fingers across it, surrounding it with tall chimneys which blotted out the blueness from its skies, and sending noisy tram-cars clanging down the Rise under the very windows of the stolid old houses, but meanwhile Thornley stubbornly survived.

Belonging to the old Hall were a few starved-looking fields with a muddy stream running through them. It was a good place for a game when their errands were done. "Look!" cried Kit, as they came to a low bridge over the stream. "Look yonder. Black Nigel hath betrayed us."

A blue-clad butcher's boy was cycling carelessly down the path, his hand on his hip and a grass stalk between his teeth. Pony looked at him keenly, shading her eyes with her hand. "Redcoats," she muttered. "Quick, under the bridge!" She was Prince Charlie, of course: she was always the Prince when they played Highlanders.

Under the bridge they crept, the black mud squelching through their sandals. The butcher's boy was followed by a couple of gossiping women with their prams. "Canst hear the rumble of their baggage wagons?" whispered Kit, when they had passed out of hearing. "Do let's get out of this. It's beastly smelly, and my feet are sopping wet."

Cautiously they emerged from their hiding-place. There was nobody in sight. "Too soon, Angus, too soon," yelled Pony. "Here comes the rearguard."

A furious fight took place at each end of the bridge. The air was thick with imaginary foes. The Redcoats were wiped out, of course: they always were. But the Prince and his followers crawled out on to the grass in a dire condition. For a few minutes their drooping figures lay prone and spent, until at length Pony jumped up impatiently. "Now, it's six months afterwards and we're all better," she cried. "What about that cake, Kit? Angus, hast thou a bannock in thy sporran?"

They followed the stream through three fields, each of which held possibilities of adventure. The first was given over to grass, and there they attacked a fortress at the gate, by swarming up an old elm tree and dropping down upon the enemy with fearsome yells. Blackened from head to foot by the sooty bark, they pressed forward to the next field, only to find an army of Redcoats in possession. They crept along the narrow pathway, speaking in stifled whispers for fear of wary sentinels, until they reached the gate and climbed over it cautiously, without a sound. The last field raised high hopes, for two old cart-horses were grazing in one corner.

These, however, flatly refused to figure as faithful steeds, whereupon the three adventurers, finding their iron-shod hoofs somewhat formidable at close range, denounced them roundly as Sassenachs and swore that they would ride no "treacherous southron mounts."

Pony turned away and, flinging her imaginary plaid about her shoulders, led the others on to where the stream flowed through a gap in the wall into the park, once part of the grounds of Thornley Old Hall. The gap was protected by spiked railings and barbed wire, but the wall, though forbidding, looked scalable. "This is our last chance of escape," said Prince Charlie firmly.

"We are ready, sire," rejoined Helen stoutly. "Only you'd better get up first, Pony. You're biggest."

Tense silence reigned for a few minutes until, grubbier than ever, the three comrades sat along the top of the wall and inspected the surrounding country. Immediately before them was a copse of stunted trees, through which they could see the level greenness of the park, crossed and re-crossed by gravel paths and patched by flower beds. Beyond rose the gabled roof of the old Hall, half-hidden by poplars, and beyond that they could just see the spire of the church at the top of the Rise. The striking of the church clock broke in upon their meditations. One.

"One o'clock!" shrieked Pony, leaping from the wall. "I shall be late for dinner and it's chicken."

Helen jumped down after her with a rueful smile on her face. "It's all right for you, but I shall get into no end of a row."

Kit did not follow them. It was a big jump and she dreaded it. A cold feeling crept over her, till it seemed as if she had been sitting up there alone for ages.

"Come on, silly, jump!" commanded Pony.

Kit looked down at her friend for a moment. Obviously she was getting impatient. Her upper lip was beginning to curl, and that always meant trouble for somebody. Yet it wasn't anything to do with her really. Kit wasn't bound to follow her. In the angle of the wall, a little farther on, stood a gnarled hawthorn tree. If only she could manage to keep her balance on the sharp-edged coping stone, she could reach it, swing herself into the upper branches, and scramble down. That would mean a new tree climbed, and it would be her own way, not Pony's. Why shouldn't she go her own way, after all?

"I'm coming! Wait a jiff!" she cried. Her feet gripped the coping stone unerringly.

"Look out, Kit! You'll fall," warned Helen.

"No, I shan't," laughed Kit, as she reached her goal in triumph. "This is a good tree, but no end prickly."

Pony eyed her enviously, but a little anxiously. It would never do for Kit to start taking the lead. "Quick, lest the Redcoats find us!" she cried, and they were back in the story-world again. Swiftly they raced across the park, sheltering behind the trees at every sign of a disguised Redcoat, on to the great gates, and beyond to the foot of the Rise. Pony and Helen wheeled to the left, after hasty farewells, and Kit went on alone, instinctively dodging passers-by as suspected Sassenachs. As she reached the gate, the dinner gong sounded noisily. Laura was waiting for her on the front doorstep.

"Late again, Kit, and filthy dirty," she exclaimed. "Whatever do Mrs. Cray and Mrs. Edgington say, I should like to know? Run upstairs at once and wash yourself. Your father's waiting."

But Kit's thoughts were still far away, roving over the Highlands of Scotland with her chief, while in the background lurked the disturbing memory of that loneliness on the top of the wall.

2. *The Red Rose*

THEY NEVER called Kit by her Christian name. In the confusion after her mother's death, she had been registered as Jane Kitson Haverard, and then, when she had grown from an ailing baby into a thin, big-eyed child, the family had discovered that nobody wanted to call her Jane, still less Janey. It still hurt too much. Richard had solved the problem by inventing "Kit," and everybody had welcomed the idea. If the child had promised to be at all like her mother, it might have been different. The Professor sometimes felt as though Janey's longed-for little daughter had died with her. Perhaps he would understand her better as she grew older. Meanwhile, it was surely best to leave her entirely to his capable young niece.

Laura thought it would have been so nice for her uncle if only Kit had been musical, like Janey. The boys did not seem to be musical, but that did not matter very much, in Laura's opinion, though of course she had done her best to encourage them in that direction. Richard could hardly distinguish one note from another, but he was the clever one, and clever people do not need to be musical. Tom refused to have pianoforte lessons because he said he wanted to play the clarinet, which was a ridiculous idea, so Laura thought. Miles could never be bothered to practice but he was very good at games, which was a much healthier interest for a boy, besides making him very popular at Marston, the great Quaker boarding-school to which all three boys had been sent.

Some day, Kit would go to boarding-school too, to Heryot Friends' School for Girls, where Laura herself had been educated. Laura thought it would do her good. She was getting far too dreamy and inattentive, and there was an obstinate streak in her which annoyed Laura very much. All this fuss about her practicing was a flagrant example of it. Laura was sure that Kit could have played the piano quite nicely if she had only tried. There had been a time when Laura had taken pride in pointing her out as the musical member of the family: the little thing had even been known to creep downstairs in her nightie on one of Laura's "musical evenings" and crouch, shivering, outside the drawing-room door. Once she had peeped in while Daisy Trimble was singing, and Daisy had been very much pleased and touched. Yet from the time she began her pianoforte lessons with Miss Miggs, all this early promise had faded away. It could not be the fault of Miss Miggs. She was the best teacher for children in Thornley, and Pony Cray did very well with her.

Miss Miggs was placid and plump, with smooth bands of mousy hair and slightly protruding eyes. Kit thought she was like a fish. During the lessons, when she was not playing secret pretending-games, Kit would make up poems about her:

> *I wish*
> *You were a fish*

On a plate,
Because I hate
The way you play
And the things you say,
And your face
Is like a plaice,
Miss Miggs!

Miss Miggs relieved the tedium of her exercises with little books of "pieces" in bright covers. Kit was stuck at *Dolly's Day* long after Pony had been promoted to *Harlequin's Party*.

"Music is dull," Kit would say, as she threw *Dolly's Day* into the farthest corner of the room.

"Kit is not musical," Miss Miggs would decide, as she wrote "Practice again, hands separately" for the twentieth time.

It was obvious to everybody that Kit was not interested in music. Sometimes the child had odd ideas about it, but then, she was always having odd ideas about things. One day she even asked if she might go to one of the Chesterham Symphony Orchestra concerts, but the notion was discouraged. "You wouldn't understand it, dear," said Laura. In any case, nobody wanted to take her. It was no use grumbling to Pony and Helen. Helen was utterly uninterested in music. Pony, on the other hand, seemed to know too much about it. "Of course you don't understand," she would say, "but it's different for us. We're musical, you see." Kit made no further comment, but she felt rebellious and puzzled. Pony seemed to have all the chances. Not that Kit coveted her position of favor with Miss Miggs. Pony could thump away at her pupils' concerts from now until Domesday, for all she cared. But it must be jolly decent to have parents who took you to the *Messiah* every Christmas as a matter of course.

"It's all very well for you," she said to Pony once. "You can go to symphony concerts whenever you like."

"Don't be so silly!" replied Pony patronizingly. "I go to the *Messiah*, but that's different. I don't want to go to a real symphony concert yet. I'd rather wait till I can really understand it."

On the first day of Kit's Easter holidays, Tom looked into the drawing-room with the remark: "I see there's an opera company at the Pavilion this week. They're doing *Carmen* tonight. I've always wanted to see it. Anyone coming?"

There was no answer, until at last Laura looked up from her library book. "Sorry, Tom, I couldn't possibly, I've got a committee. What about Miles?"

"Sorry again!" grinned Miles. "Not my idea of fun!"

Tom hesitated. He hated going to the theatre by himself, but there seemed to be nothing else for it. His father would certainly not want to go, and Richard was still at Oxford. Suddenly he caught sight of Kit, curled up as usual in the corner of the sofa. "Look here, why shouldn't I take the kid?" he suggested.

"Kit!" exclaimed Laura. "Kit! Why! she's far too young to enjoy it. It isn't even as if she were musical. She'll only be bored stiff. And in any case, it's much too late."

"Oh, Laura, please," wailed Kit.

"School tomorrow," snapped Laura.

"No, it isn't! You know it isn't. Do let me go."

"I can't help it—" Laura was beginning, when her protest was scotched by the Professor himself. He laid aside his *Chesterham Guardian*, knocked the ash off his cigar, and suddenly came out with the amazing statement: "My dear Laura, surely the child is growing up now?"

As a matter of fact, the Professor had not the slightest idea of his daughter's age. She might have been anything from seven to seventeen, so far as he knew. Nevertheless, his intervention settled the matter, if only because it was so unexpected. Laura ventured one last protest. "I'm sure it isn't at all suitable for her," she declared.

"Isn't it really, dear?" asked the Professor in dismay. "What is it about?"

"I don't exactly know, Uncle," confessed Laura. "I've never seen it."

"Oh, come on, be a sport, Laura!" protested Miles from his corner. "Let the kid go, for once. She won't understand a word of it anyhow."

Laura shrugged her shoulders. They were all against her, so she might as well give in. After all, it did not really matter very much. "Very well," she declared at last. "You may go, Kit. Only don't say I didn't warn you, that's all. Hurry up and get your things on, child. You mustn't keep Tom waiting."

Kit bounded upstairs, singing at the top of her voice.

"Oh, Kit! *do* stop making that awful noise," called Laura. "I simply can't stand it."

"Sorry!" shouted Kit. "I just couldn't help it. I'm so happy!"

"Well, try being happy quietly," suggested Laura. "Some of us want to read."

It did not take Kit long to get ready. As she was scrubbing the dirt from her hands, she began to sing again. The bathroom was such a jolly place to make a row in, when you were feeling happy. She hit the tune of the folk-song they were learning at school. "The lark in the morn she will rise up from her nest"—but it wasn't the morn, it was after teatime, and she was going to stay up late. "And mount up in the air with the dew all on her breast"—oh bother! She had made dirty marks all over the towel. Never mind, Laura wouldn't see them until after she had gone. She slammed the bathroom door and began to race downstairs two steps at a time. "And like the pretty ploughboy she will whistle and will sing"—she caught Laura's eye as she reached the drawing-room door and stopped abruptly. "Sorry, Laura!" she said.

"I should hope so!" rejoined Laura indignantly. "You might have a little consideration for the rest of the family. It's a pity you haven't got a nice little voice like Daisy Trimble. Then perhaps we should be *asking* you to sing."

Kit hesitated. Perhaps she didn't want to go out so very much after all. But Tom caught her by the arm and hustled her to the front door. "Buck up, kid, or we'll miss the tram!" he said. He kept hold of her arm as they hurried to the tram-stop on the Rise. Tom never said very much, but he was a good sort, thought Kit.

She was far too excited to talk on the way into Chester-ham. It all seemed too good to be true. Only the day before Pony had been telling her that of course she would not go to the Opera with her parents, as she wasn't old enough to appreciate it yet! How Kit would enjoy telling her all about it—if only she would not be superior and disapprove of her for having gone. But somehow or other, nowadays, it did not seem to matter quite so much what Pony thought about things.

They waited for some time in the queue for the "Extra Early Pit." Now and again Tom would look down with a smile. "Keep your pecker up, kid!" he encouraged her. "We'll soon be in."

Kit did not mind the long wait. It was all part of the fun.

When at last the queue moved into the theatre, they triumphantly secured good seats in the middle of a row, almost
immediately behind the stalls. Then came an even longer
wait, while the theatre slowly filled up, but she spent the
time very happily, reading her program and watching the
newcomers. When one by one the members of the orchestra
began to arrive, Tom's patience was tried almost to breaking
point by her rapid fire of questions. "Why are they making
that noise? . . . What's that man playing? . . . What do they
tune by? . . . Why—"

"Oh, shut up, kid!" protested Tom at last. "Folk are looking round."

The conductor entered, amidst loud applause. Kit could
not resist another attack. "Why do they have a conductor?
. . . Does he have to know how to play all the instruments?
. . . How—"

"Sh!" whispered Tom. "Do for goodness' sake dry up!
They're starting."

The conductor rapped the desk: the overture began. Kit
sat motionless, lost in a new world. At the first strains of the
"Toreador Song" she started, like a hunter at the huntsman's
horn.

"That's the 'Toreador Song,'"whispered Tom. "It comes
in again later."

She did not hear him. Had she done so, it would have
been her turn to whisper "Dry up!"

The busy opening scene was exciting, but a little puzzling.
It was such a long time before anything happened. She liked
the music and the bright costumes, but she could not get the
hang of things. Then, suddenly, nothing mattered any more,
nothing but a vision of a black-haired girl in a long-fringed
Spanish shawl, a girl with magic fire in her eyes and a red

rose in her mouth—Carmen! Carmen!

From that moment Kit lived in the world on the stage. It was a world which expressed itself in music, but she found nothing strange in that: it was almost as if she recognized a common tongue. The story was a little involved, but it was quite easy to understand, so she told Pony and Helen afterwards. "There was Carmen, you see, and she was so wonderful that they all fell in love with her. And she was going to marry a soldier called Don José, only I can't think why, because he was awfully stupid and kept on making a mess of things. I should have chosen the Toreador, if I'd been she. He was much nicer and nothing like so fat. They went off to a sort of gypsy camp with the smugglers, and old José didn't fit in a bit. I bet he hated camping out. The Toreador came too, and they were going to fight—there'd have been some sense in that—but then a silly little woman came trailing after Don José with a message from his mother and he went away with her. P'r'aps it was the best thing he could have done, but he might have gone home and stayed there, instead of—"

Kit could not describe the last scene. She could not understand that culminating tragedy. She had seen Carmen hold the stage like a queen, her proud head crowned with the lace mantilla, and then Don José had come slinking in, ragged and unshaven, and looking fatter than ever. Perhaps he wanted to kneel at Carmen's feet and ask forgiveness. She could not catch the words. But why did Carmen edge away from him? Surely there was nothing for her to fear?—Ah! What was that? The flash of a knife. A little sob burst from Kit's throat as Carmen of the red rose sank like a wounded bird to lie, lifeless and beautiful, on the dusty stage.

The lights flared in a thunder of applause. Kit sat on until Tom jerked her to her feet. She busied herself in gathering her things together, forcing back her tears, for fear lest he should see them and be ashamed of her. She said no word, nor did she break her silence during the ride home on the tram-car. But as they waited on the threshold, she whispered hurriedly: "I say, Tom, thanks awfully! Thanks just ever so!"

"Did she enjoy it?" asked Laura curiously.

"I suppose so," was the illuminating reply. "Odd kid!"

3. *"The Year's at the Spring"*

SOMETIMES KIT would stop suddenly in the middle of her homework and sit with her elbows on the table, chewing her pencil stub and trying to think things out. Everything seemed different nowadays: even Pony and Helen could not understand. How she longed for a "best friend." Pony always had one. It was not always the same girl, of course, but she was never without a "very best." Kit would have envied Pony if she had not been so proud of her.

In the old days, when she had been content to follow Pony's leadership unquestioningly, how much simpler life had been. Once she even approached Pony herself upon the subject. "I wish I was popular at school, like you. I don't seem to get on somehow."

Pony hesitated. She did not want to hurt her friend, but really, Kit had been rather impossible lately. "It's your own fault for being such an odd fish," she said. "Why can't you buck up and do something? Why don't you play games?"

Inevitably Kit flashed out and there was a squabble. "Odd fish yourself! It's you that's getting too beastly cocky."

"Cocky? What about you, always going round with your head in the air?"

"Oh, leave me alone!"

"Well, what did you ask me for?"

Afterwards, the adjective returned to her memory, "Odd." That was what Tom had said after *Carmen*. And last vacation she had overheard Laura saying to Richard: "Yes, she's coming on, isn't she? But it's a pity she's such an *odd* child." What on earth did they all mean? It was horrid of them to talk about her like that: she must jolly well find some way of showing them that she was no more odd than they were.

Helen, quite unconsciously, suggested the remedy. She had come early one Sunday morning to pick up Kit on the way to the Quaker Meeting which they all attended. They were strolling along the pavement, waiting for Pony. Helen had a handful of humbugs loose in her blazer pocket.

"I wish you were in my class," said she.

"Why on earth?" asked Kit, with her mouth full.

"Oh, it's rotten, not having either you or Pony," was the reply. "It wasn't so bad when Pony and I were together, but now she's down among the betas, and I scarcely ever see her. And she'll be going to Heryot soon. Anyhow, she's got such piles of friends. She's awfully popular, you know."

"But haven't you got piles of friends?"

"Oh, I like lots of girls," said Helen, "but I don't want them to bother me. You're different."

"Pity I can't get a double remove," observed Kit, sucking thoughtfully.

"You could," rejoined Helen dryly, "if you won the Junior Medal."

"Me!" exclaimed Kit. "Me! The Junior Medal!"

"Why not?"

"But you don't know, Helen. My arithmetic's awful!"

"Is that all? I shouldn't let that stop me."

"Hm! But Helen, you never let anything stop you,

do you?"

"Perhaps not." A resolute spirit shone behind Helen's spectacles. "I had a row at home, the other day," she said slowly. She seldom spoke of home, even to her two friends.

"What was it about?" asked Kit curiously.

"Mother wants me to leave the High School and go to Penart Close with Marjory and Millicent."

Kit pictured Helen's pretty sisters: they used to dance with Miles sometimes in the holidays, but Richard and Tom couldn't stand them. "But why——?" she began.

"I'm Mother's disappointment, you know!" said Helen with a wry smile. "Perhaps she thinks Penart will improve me."

"What did you say?"

"I said I wouldn't go. I shouldn't mind going to Heryot with Pony, but I'm not going to play about at a fashion-plate school for anybody. Anyhow, what on earth's the use of making Daddy shell out the fees for Penart, when nothing on earth will make me as pretty as the others, which is all Mother wants."

Kit thought of Professor Edgington, with his stammer and his fussy little ways. "What did your father say?" she asked.

Helen shook her head. "He just said: 'I don't know, Maggie dear, I don't know!' And that wasn't much use, you see, because Mother loathes being called Maggie. But I went on sticking to it and in the end he backed me up. Only I do hate rows."

"Helen! Kit! Wait a jiffy, I'm coming," called Pony in the distance. She was racing up the Rise, her long legs flying under her Sunday frock. Helen fished up another couple of humbugs and gave one to Kit, who carefully pulled off the fluff before popping it into her mouth.

"I say, Helen, I shall try for the Junior Medal," she said.

"Then you'll probably win it," observed Helen.

"I say!" broke in Pony as she panted up, "we'll be jolly late if we don't look out. I nearly waited to go in the car with the others."

They walked to Meeting from choice. The old Friends' Meeting House was in the center of the city, near the Jubilee Square. It was a dull walk, but they knew every short cut, and nearly every hiding-place: it was a glorious opportunity for pretending-games.

"Come on!" urged Pony. "I'm Prince Charlie and the Meeting House is Skye. Hurry up!"

"Minnie Calendar's taking our class today, isn't she?" interrupted Kit abruptly.

"Yes, worse luck. Why?"

"Oh, dunno! Only I wish we hadn't got to go. I can't stand the sound of her voice. She meows at us."

"Silly! What do people's voices matter?" laughed Pony. "Let's get on with the game."

Kit promptly reeled against a hoarding. "The Redcoats! The Redcoats!" she cried.

Racing along the dusty pavement, they were back in the other world again. When they reached the bridge over the canal, they paused for breath. "Why should we go to the children's class, anyways?" asked Helen suddenly.

Pony turned to her in astonishment. "Oh, but Helen, we couldn't stay away from Meeting!" she exclaimed.

"I don't see why not," mused Helen. "But that's not what I meant. I'm getting fed up with the children's class. Why shouldn't we go straight into the big Meeting?"

"I say, do let's!" cried Kit, longing to get away from Minnie Calendar's mew. "After all, you know, the children's class is only grown-ups jawing at us. It's nothing to do with us really. They're always telling us about the Early Quaker children, and how the kids at Reading held Meeting while their parents were in prison, but they never give *us* a chance."

"Oh! it must have been grand fun then," said Pony eagerly, jerking the hair out of her eyes with the quick toss of her head which had given her her nickname. "I wish it was like that now, and the Redcoats would break into the Meeting. Wouldn't I just fight 'em?"

"No, you wouldn't," interrupted Helen coolly. "You'd be a Quaker, so you couldn't. But if we don't hurry up, we'll never get anywhere. Come on, let's run!"

They ran silently, keeping stolidly in step, under the dark walls of the warehouses and across the empty streets, till they reached the granite waste of the Jubilee Square. Here they wheeled about, and so raced the last few hundred yards, halting finally beneath the portico of the Friends' Meeting House.

"We're late," panted Pony.

"Come on!" whispered Kit, hitching up her stockings. "Let's go into the big Meeting and sit at the back."

Somewhat disheveled and out of breath, they pushed through the doorway of the silent room. At least one shoe squeaked. Several bowed heads were raised at the disturbance, but it was soon over, and as the children settled down nervously on one of the back benches, all was quiet again.

It was some time before Kit ventured to raise her head and look about her. She soon saw Laura, sitting in her usual place and, she felt quite sure from the rigid silhouette, entirely disapproving of this untimely appearance. (The children were even now raising their voices in "All things bright and beautiful," after which they were doomed to half an hour of Minnie Calendar. She was better where she was!) Her father was away, but both Professor and Mrs. Edgington were there, and Dr. and Mrs. Cray were "facing the Meeting," on the elders' benches. Kit liked to look at Mrs. Cray; she always wore such pretty hats.

Gradually her thoughts began to be drawn into the silence. She no longer looked about her, but rested her chin upon her hand and so fell into that absolute stillness which is the heritage of all Quaker children. For a while the pretending-game engrossed her. All the people around her were Redcoats and discovery meant death. Her mind flashed back to the adventures of yesterday. They had played in Thornley Hall fields again, only this time they had not gone back over the wall. Pony had taken a dislike to that way now. The whole world had seemed bathed in sunshine, and the fields had been sweet with the smell of hawthorn blossom. Spring was breaking into summer, and surely this had been the loveliest spring of all. What was it she had read the other day?

> *The year's at the spring,*
> *And day's at the morn;*
> *Morning's at seven;*
> *The hillside's dew-pearled;*

It had been like that this morning too. She had felt like singing all the way along the road. Things were so different in spring. There were even sunbeams in the Meeting House, striking through the dusty windows and painted flatly along the empty gallery. They shone along the row of "elders," sparkling on Spencer Carew's watch chain and Anna Maria Trimble's chatelaine, and lighting up the kindly, contemplative faces of the Friends.

The silence grew still deeper until, striking heavily across it, came the dull boom of the Town Hall clock, eleven strokes so slow and ponderous that Kit almost failed to count them. As the last one died away, there was a slight stir. A deep voice rang out: "Friends, we are called upon to bear great responsibilities in these dark days."

Joseph Garth Fenwick had risen from his seat. His tall figure was slightly bent and his great hands rested on the back of the form in front of him. Kit liked the rich tones of his voice, but somehow he seemed to bring back the shadows into the Meeting House.

Her thoughts wandered away again, up into the patch of sunlit sky which glittered beyond the fast-shut casements. A wisp of white cloud sailed across, like a tiny ship. Supposing it was a ship, and she the captain, venturing new countries in the skies. Supposing—

"Dark clouds have gathered around us, Friends, and there are days when we can scarce see the Way before us."

But what a silly thing to think on a day like this. Kit preferred Browning—

> God's in his Heaven—
> All's right with the world!

Joseph Garth Fenwick spoke at length. He generally did. Kit was pretending that they were all Early Friends and he was preaching to them in prison, when suddenly she caught his closing words: "We are called to hard work and suffering, to sorrow and tribulation, to unsparing sacrifice in the service of the Truth."

The broken silence was caught together again. She shifted in her seat and looked around. Why didn't somebody get up and say what a jolly morning it was, with the blue sky and sunshine, and God behind it all somehow, just wanting everybody to enjoy it? That's what she would have said, if she had been a grown-up, or if she had been an Early Quaker child, for that matter. The idea which had been lurking in the back of her mind flashed into view—why not? Why not? Her thoughts raced to and fro. Why should not she get up and recite "The year's at the spring"? She could recite a deal better than Anna Maria Trimble anyhow, and she was always saying bits of poetry in Meeting. How surprised they would all be. She looked round at Pony and Helen: they were obviously deep in pretending-games. She wondered if they could hear her heart thumping. It had begun to beat furiously.

Suddenly she saw old Nicholas Hayman frowning, which meant that he would speak soon, and then her chance would be gone. It must be now or never—now! She sprang to her feet, gripping the form in front of her, in imitation of Joseph Garth Fenwick, saw a white wave of surprised faces break upon the stillness of the Meeting, saw Laura half-rise in her seat and Mrs. Cray smile a little anxiously, and said—nothing. The silence surged up around her, bore down upon her, choking her, until she stood dumbly before them all, a dishevelled, frightened little girl. She looked round helplessly. Laura, tight-lipped, beckoned to her firmly to sit down. It was like being on the top of the wall, she thought. And with that reminder, her fear vanished. She looked up to the row of windows above the gallery. The little white cloud had gone, but the window panes were glittering in the

sunlight, and outside everything would be fresh and green and laughing, not bleak and cold and miserable, like Joseph Garth Fenwick's world.

> *The year's at the spring,*
> *And day's at the morn;*
> *Morning's at seven;*
> *The hillside's dew-pearled;*
> *The lark's on the wing;*
> *The snail's on the thorn:*
> *God's in his heaven—*
> *All's right with the world!*

Her voice rang out clearly in the stillness; then, with a little sigh, she slid back into her seat.

The rustle which signified the close of the Meeting came as a surprise somehow. For once, the time had passed almost too quickly. Kit fled before anybody could stop her. "Come on, let's walk back—quick!" she called to Pony and Helen, who came panting after her.

"Why on earth—?" began Pony, but Helen stopped her with a nudge. Together they slipped away and walked for a while in silence. "Let's pretend!" cried Kit at last, whereupon they all took refuge in that other world of theirs, the only sanctuary they knew.

At the gate of Thornley Mays they paused. "Will—will Laura be back?" asked Pony.

"I saw her go past on the top of a tram," said Helen.

Kit, her hand on the gate, stood kicking the bottom bar. She looked very small.

"Cheerio!" cried Pony. "And don't forget you're coming to us for tea."

"If *she* lets me," rejoined Kit darkly. Squaring her shoulders, she turned about and marched resolutely up the path.

Laura was waiting for her. "Well, Kit?" said she.

"What's up?" enquired Kit, with studied carelessness.

"Now, it's no use pretending you don't know perfectly well. Pretending, indeed! It's time someone put a stop to your pretending. It's all very well making sillies of yourselves and misbehaving in the streets, but when it comes to making mock of sacred things—"

"But Laura, I didn't! I—"

"Yes, you did. You can't deny it. I knew perfectly well when I saw you three children come in together, that you'd got some silly game on between yourselves. Why weren't you in the children's class?"

"We thought—we didn't want—"

"Didn't want, indeed! As if that had anything to do with it, when we trust you to go to Meeting properly by yourselves. I see we shall have to take you like babies. But how you had the face to behave as you did, I can't think. I never did such a thing, when I was your age."

"P'r'aps not! But truly, Laura, it wasn't just a game. Why, Mrs. Cray spoke afterwards and she said—"

"Mrs. Cray came to the rescue very well, but that doesn't say you weren't a naughty little girl."

The phrase stung like a whiplash. "You're a beast, Laura," cried Kit, stamping her foot. "Lemme go!"

As she raced upstairs, a cool voice followed her. "Wash your face and come down quickly. Dinner's nearly ready."

"Shan't!"

"Do you hear what I say?"

"Don't want any dinner."

"Do you want me to come and fetch you?"

There was silence for a while, until Kit slammed the bathroom door and came slowly downstairs. It was not a cheerful meal, though Laura, having won her point, made some attempt at brisk conversation.

"Can I go now?"

"Yes, you may."

The rebel force retired in good order, with a moment's hesitation at the door. Would a good slam be worth while? No, it would almost certainly lead to further humiliation. Kit conducted her retreat to a successful conclusion, raced upstairs, banged her own door, locked it, and flung herself face downwards on her bed.

Footsteps came to the door and went away again, Laura's swift and light, Martha's heavy and comforting. After a while a horn sounded in front of the house, the bell rang, and a big voice echoed in the hall. "Doctor Cray," muttered Kit. "And Laura will say I can't go to tea. Don't care! Don't want to!"

Suddenly she heard his firm tread on the staircase. "Hullo! Hullo!" he called. "Is there a little maid anywhere who wants to come for a run?"

She flew to the door. He mustn't find it locked. And he mustn't see how red her eyes were. She snatched up her damp face-cloth and rubbed it over her face. There was no time for more; the door burst open and the big doctor strode in. "Well now, this is jolly! I've a case out at Favering and it's a glorious afternoon. Hurry up and get ready!"

"Did Laura say I could?" asked Kit incredulously.

"Of course she did! Come along and don't waste any more of this lovely afternoon."

There was no resisting the Doctor in this mood. It seemed almost no time before she was waving a hesitant good-bye to

Laura from the front seat of the car. Contrary to her fears, he did not talk at all on the way out to Favering. Little by little, her eyes stopped smarting and the queer ache left her throat, until she was able to look about her. She was beginning to enjoy herself, whether she would or no.

The Doctor's visit did not take long. He soon came hurrying out to rejoin her. "Well, well, nothing serious after all!" he exclaimed. "But we've had a jolly run, and now I must drive like a spot of greased lightning, or Pony will haul me over the coals for running away with you."

On the way homewards, Kit suddenly made up her mind. "Doctor—" she began.

"Yes, my dear?" said he quietly.

"Was it wrong to speak in Meeting?"

The Doctor slowed up a little. "No, my dear," he replied. "Why should it be?"

"Laura said I was making mock of sacred things."

"And were you?"

"Of course I wasn't!"

"Then that's all right, my dear."

"How can it be? How do you know?"

"If it wasn't all right, little maid, wouldn't you be feeling very unhappy inside?"

"Y-yes, I suppose I should."

"Well, that's the thing to go by. That's what the old Quakers meant when they talked about the 'Light Within.' Even if they had to go against all the powers that were, they didn't mind, so long as they felt happy about it inside. If they weren't quite sure about it, they'd wait quietly until they were—'waiting upon God,' they called it—but when once they were certain, nothing could stop them."

Kit hesitated. "It must be rather nice to feel so sure about things," she said, "instead of being all muddled up. That's what I usually feel like, as if there were a kind of real me inside that couldn't get out. But you seem to think that's God, which sounds a bit sort of funny to me."

"Perhaps we're both right, my dear," suggested the Doctor.

They did not talk again until they reached the outskirts of Thornley. As they were passing the boundary wall of the park, Kit wriggled uneasily in her seat. "You know, it was all a bit mixed up this morning," she confessed. "I suppose Laura was right in a way. It did begin as a kind of pretend-ing-game. And I thought I could manage as well as some of the old fogies who get up and jaw. But afterwards—it was different. Only I can't explain."

"Don't try to!" advised the Doctor, swinging round by the park gates. "I'm not particularly good at it myself. But remember, little maid, nothing worth while ever grows in a hurry, not even your 'real me,' as you call it. That's why your cousin Laura was so upset. But sometimes it takes you unawares, and that's why you were able to give us a bit of sense this morning. Now don't worry any more: we're nearly home and I can see Pony waiting for us at the gate."

Kit turned to him as she scrambled out of the car. "Thanks awfully, Doctor," she said, and then raced up the path.

Pony was waiting for her with a dirty face; an old overall covered her Sunday frock. "Hullo, Kit! I thought you were never coming," she said.

"Where's Helen?" asked Kit.

"Oh, she came ages ago. We're exploring up in the attic. We've found a little door where you can get right under the rafters, but you must be careful where you tread or you go through the spare-room ceiling. Hurry up! Just throw your things down any old where."

Kit raced upstairs after Pony. Muffled shouts from Helen were coming from somewhere under the roof.

"All right, Kit's here!" bellowed Pony. "Don't go any farther till we come."

"Wait for us, Helen," shouted Kit, as she panted up the stairs to the attic.

Helen's face, streaked with dirt, appeared at the little door. "What about your frock?" she asked. "It's rather dusty up here."

"Oh, never mind about her frock!" declared Pony impatiently. "Come on!" She clambered hastily through the little door, bringing down a shower of dust and cobwebs. She did not want Helen to be the first to explore. Kit followed obediently as usual. It did matter about her frock, whatever Pony might think. There would be no end of a row with Laura. But it was no use bothering; unlike the row this morning, it would not be about anything serious.

Downstairs, the Doctor had come in from the garage to find his wife encamped in the drawing-room with the younger children and an overflowing mending basket.

"Well?" she queried, smiling up at him.

"All's well, my dear!" said he.

4. *Martha*

"HOW OLD ARE you, Martha?" asked Kit suddenly one evening. She was sitting in the big wicker armchair in the kitchen, with a generous slice of bread pudding, and the mug of milk which Martha insisted on her taking nowadays at bedtime. ("That child wants feeding up, Miss Laura," Martha had declared. "I don't hold with all these examinations.") Jemima, the great ginger tom-cat, settled down contently on her knee with his paws tucked in and purred drowsily, soothed by an occasional caress about his ears. Kit leaned back among the cushions. "How old are you, Martha?" she repeated.

There had been a time when Martha would have scorned to answer such a question, but just now Kit occupied a favored place. "Fifty-five, my dear," she replied, holding up a stocking to inspect a network of darns.

"Fifty-five. Is that very old?"

"Well, I still seem to be able to hobble along, don't I?"

"Yes. But, Martha, Father was sixty last birthday. How did you manage to be Mother's nurse if you're younger than Father?"

"Why, dearie, that isn't to say your mother would have been sixty now if she'd lived, poor lamb. She was twenty years younger than Professor Haverard."

"Oh, I see. Go on, Martha. Tell me how you came to be her nurse."

Martha hesitated. Laura had always discouraged her from talking to Kit about Janey. ("I have to take her mother's place, you see," she would explain. "You mustn't make it difficult for me.") Martha threaded her darning needle and went on. "Well, I was in service with your great-grandmother, Mrs. Charles Kitson, at Belceaster House in Manningleigh, and so was my mother before me. It's a nice little town, is Manningleigh, very pretty and old-fashioned. Have you nearly finished your milk, dearie? Because it's time you were getting to bed."

"Oh, not yet, Martha!" pleaded Kit. "Be a sport! Tell me some more about Belceaster House. Mother had lots of aunts and uncles, hadn't she?"

"Any number of them. But they were mostly grown up and gone away by the time I went there. Miss Sophia, that was my mother's favorite, died just before I was born: they called me Martha Sophia after her—not that I ever use the name. She was the eldest, and they all thought a lot of her, though Miss Susan, who married Mr. Mark Spurrier of Middlehampton, was by far the prettiest."

"Weren't there any boys?" asked Kit.

"Why, yes. I never met Mr. Frederick—he'd gone abroad before my time—and Mr. Charles was married and living in Belceaster. That's a nice place too, with a big Cathedral and any number of queer old nooks and corners. He and your grandfather, Mr. Philip, ran the old family business with their Uncle Shillitoe. Grocers and tea merchants, they were. Mr. and Mrs. Charles lived in the old house above the shop, and so did your grandfather until he married and started the branch at Belmouth. There was only Miss Henrietta and Miss Maria and Miss Priscilla left at home."

"How dull!" said Kit. "Go on, please, Martha."

Martha folded up the neatly mended stockings and took out her knitting. "I don't know what there is to tell," said she. "I liked best the times when the grandchildren came: I was always fond of children."

"Tell me about Mother."

Martha hesitated for a moment, knitting steadily, and then went on. "Your mother was the prettiest baby I ever saw. And from the day I first carried a scuttle of coal up into the old nursery, she took to me like as if she would never have me leave her. She was often with us, on account of Mrs. Philip being so delicate. And when her parents had to go abroad for the winter, they left her at Belceaster House and asked me to be her nurse. I can see them now, standing in the hall before they went away—Mr. Philip so tall and handsome, and she so white and frail and lovely. We never saw them again. They were drowned together in Italy."

Martha said no more for a while. Kit sat curled up in her chair, absently stroking Jemima. Dreamily she pulled a velvet ear, until Jemima protested sleepily. "Go on about Mother," said she.

"About little Miss Janey?" Martha held up her knitting and rapidly counted the stitches. "Why, she lived with us, of course. Miss Maria took charge of her."

"Wasn't she lonely, with only grown-ups?" asked Kit.

"No, why should she be? We were never without one or other of the grandchildren. Master Charles and Miss Emily and Master Robert from Belceaster were never off the doorstep. They used to have great games together in the garden. It was such a garden as you never see in these parts, and the children might go anywhere they liked, so long as they didn't pluck the flowers or the fruit. It was all at the back of the house. There wasn't any garden in front. The door opened straight on to the Place, and if the back door was open, you could see right through to the first lawn, and smell the flowers and the roses."

"It all sounds so lovely, Martha. Did they play pretending-games?"

"To be sure they did, though they didn't go gallivanting round like you do. Children were brought up more strictly then, you know, and I can't see it did them any harm. But even when she had none of her cousins to play with, Miss Janey would be busy with little games of her own, and sometimes she would tell me about them, and sometimes she wouldn't. And I would often hear her singing to herself in the garden, when she thought none of us were about. She had a pretty voice even then: it's a pity none of you take after her."

Kit sat up in her chair and clasped her knees, thereby greatly upsetting the dignity of Jemima. "Martha!" she said abruptly. "I want to go to Manningleigh."

Martha looked steadfastly down at her knitting. "Why, dearie?" she asked.

"I want to see that garden. I want to see the places where Mother used to play."

"But that was all so long ago: maybe it's altered now. You'd find it dull perhaps. There's no children and no young ladies any more."

"But they're not *all* dead, Martha, are they?"

There was a sharp note in Kit's voice. Martha laid by her knitting. "No, no, dearie, of course not!" she reassured her. "But you wouldn't like an old-fashioned house in a left-behind country town, and none but old ladies to talk to."

"I think I should. I know I would. I *want* to go, Martha."

Kit's eyes were shining, her face flushed. Martha eyed her with alarm. "There, there, don't take on so! After all, why shouldn't you go? You would have gone there long ago, if I'd had my way, but it's no use crying over spilt milk. What makes you so interested, all at once?"

"Dunno!" mumbled Kit. Her excitement had died down and she looked tired and pale.

Martha glanced at the clock. "Why, how time's flown!" she exclaimed. "I ought to have packed you off to bed long ago. I must be getting supper ready. Run along, there's a good girl. Miss Laura'll be back soon."

Kit pushed Jemima off her knee and kissed Martha goodnight. It was no use trying to put off bedtime any longer. Martha had already swept her mug and plate into the scullery sink, and the bustle of supper preparations was in the air. She slipped into the study to say good-night to her father, but he was so hard at work that he scarcely seemed to notice her. He must be writing another book, she thought. Slowly she trailed upstairs. The upper flight was always dark and dingy, even in summer-time. Somewhere in the distance she could hear a melancholy tap dripping. It was a relief to reach the haven of her own room. The things which lurked on the staircase could never catch her there.

Shabby and untidy though it was, Kit liked her own room better than any of the others. It was furnished with "leftovers" and seldom decorated, but nothing really counted beside the fact that it was her own. Over her bed hung a faded photograph of Janey, and above the mantelpiece was an old-fashioned water-color painted in Italy long ago by

Philip Kitson. Beneath it stood Janey's pot-pourri bowl, chipped and cracked and seamed with age, and therefore despised in the drawing-room. Kit loved to lift the lid and sniff the old-world fragrance.

She hurried out of her clothes and into her pajamas. It would never do for Laura to come back from her sale of work and find her not yet in bed. She would surely be back soon, for it was nearly supper-time, and Kit knew that she was going afterwards to a committee meeting at Mrs. Cray's. Laura served on a great many committees: Kit liked them to be in the evenings, because then she could read late without anybody finding out.

The front door banged, and there was a murmuring of voices, first in the study, and then in the kitchen. Kit could hear Laura hurrying up to her room to change. It would not be a grand frock for a committee: probably the old blue spotted silk would do. The staircase creaked to swift footsteps ascending, and Kit dived beneath the bedclothes as Laura came in. "Hullo, dear! Ready for byes?" said she.

"Yes. But Laura, do stay and talk a bit."

"I mustn't. Your father's ready for supper, and I've a committee tonight. Go to sleep, ragamuffin!"

Kit snuggled down dutifully. She was not making any rash promises. She wanted to read in bed when once Laura was out of the way. "Good-night, Laura," she said.

Laura paused in the doorway. "By the way, Martha said something about your being tired after the dancing class today."

"Did she? I hate dancing anyhow! Lots of the girls don't take it, so why should I have to bother with it? Can't I stop?"

"Now, Kit, that's naughty of you. You know as well as I

do that you'll be sorry when you're older. I believe you're just having Martha on."

"No, no! It isn't that—but can't you see—"

"I can see you're a silly kid. If you didn't try to sit up all night, you wouldn't get half so tired. Now you settle down like a good child and go to sleep."

"All right!"—this very sulkily.

"Now, don't be cross!" Laura re-entered the room and bent to kiss an unresponsive cheek. "Good-night, dear."

The tap of light little heels died away in the distance. "I hate dancing," muttered Kit. But it was not really dancing that she hated. It was that "something" which Martha had noticed—"You drink this drop of milk and no nonsense. You're tired out, that's what you are"—which had caught hold of her as she toiled up the staircase, forcing her to halt awhile, panting, as she clung dizzily to the banisters.

The gong sounded, and she heard Laura and the Professor go into the dining-room. At last she was safe from disturbance. She badly wanted to read. Martha had made her hurry over her homework and she knew her sums were all wrong. Dancing-class days were always diffcult, though Laura did not seem to think so. "But you've got stacks of time, silly," she would say. "Why can't you work ahead?"

Deep in *The Prince and the Page*, Kit scarcely noticed the sounds which indicated the end of supper and Laura's departure for the committee. Little by little, the house grew very still. It was so quiet that it seemed to be listening for something. Involuntarily, against the background of her reading, Kit began to listen, too. The water-pipes gurgled suddenly and Kit held her breath for fear lest they should boil. She couldn't bear it when the water boiled in the pipes; the cistern in the bathroom would sound like some horrible monster escaping from captivity.

Suddenly she sat up with a jerk. What was that? Surely something had rustled beneath her window. She dived down under the bedclothes. What could it be? Was someone, or worse still, *something* prowling about in the shrubbery? Ever since she had been quite small, she had had a secret dread lest some day a wild animal should escape from the zoo and take refuge in the garden, or one of the snakes might come slithering in at her window. She crouched down among the blankets, scarcely daring to breathe, whilst her heart thumped warningly and the chilly sweat broke over her. All was silent again. Had she imagined it then? No, for there it was again, louder than ever. The window of the room next to hers rattled grimly. Surely no window ever rattled like that of its own accord. Could it be burglars? And if so, what should she do? If she called out, nobody would hear her. She must try to frighten them away. Suddenly she darted out of bed, slammed the door violently twice, threw her shoes with a clatter into the fender, and coughed with a masculine cough. With one flying leap she was under the blankets again, listening breathlessly. The sounds were not repeated. "Done the trick!"she chuckled, and pulled the book from under her pillow. The cat stole away from the shrubbery, and the little gust of wind which had rattled the old window-frame died down again. All was safe.

The evening wore on. Kit grew tired of reading at last and hid the book under her pillow. Laura came back late from the committee and bustled about the house, locking doors and fastening windows. One by one the grown-ups could be heard going up to bed. The Professor came last, after a mild altercation with Laura.

"Time you gave up for tonight, Uncle. Come to bed."

"Not just yet, dear. Thee run along upstairs. I'll put the lights out."

"Now, Uncle, you know you'll just go on reading till to-morrow morning if I leave you to it. And that won't do, for I can't have you tired out for the Trafford lecture."

"But—"

"Uncle, dear, *please*! Thou really must."

Laura seldom used the "plain tongue" of the Quakers; when she did, her voice softened. The Professor drew her to him and kissed her on the forehead. "Thou'rt a dear child," he said, and so suffered her to lead him upstairs.

Kit tossed to and fro. Would she never be able to go to sleep? Her sums haunted her bed like spectres, impossible fractions and rows of decimals, leaky cisterns, running bath-taps, and those indefatigable workmen, A, B and C. They were all wrong, she knew they were. If only she could get up early and do them again. She must listen for Martha's alarm clock and then creep downstairs and get her satchel. If Martha caught her, she would send her back to bed again and tell her she was too tired. Tired. What did it matter if she were tired? Surely everybody was tired sometimes. Martha was an old fusser and she'd jolly well tell her so.

How hot it was. And yet the night had seemed cold. Surely there was something funny about it. And what was that faint smell? "Is the house on fire?" she whispered, hor-ror-stricken. "Oh no, it can't be, it can't! There isn't any smell at all." She buried her face in the pillow. She *would* go to sleep. After a while she raised it again, "Coward!" she said to herself accusingly. "Coward! If the house is on fire and everybody's burned in their beds, it'll be your fault. Get up and look down the staircase—no, no, I can't—I daren't—you must—you must—get up!"

She rolled out of bed and pattered barefoot across the chill linoleum. The landing was dark and silent. She groped for the stair rail and looked down the well of the staircase. There was nothing there. All was enfolded in darkness and quiet, and the funny smell had vanished. Only, as she stood clinging to the rail, it seemed almost as if the house were holding its breath. She turned and fled back to bed.

The night wore on. How she came to be at the dancing-class in her pajamas, she could not think, but there she was, and there were all the rest in their summer frocks. A lot of other people were there besides, Laura and the boys, her father and Doctor Cray, and the Friends from the Meeting House. And they had been dancing and dancing for ages, never stopping, so that she could have cried for weariness. She would beg the other dancers to stop—"Oh, do please stop!—I can't!—I can't!"—and they would laugh in her face and whirl on in a tireless round. On and on they went, and then suddenly came to a standstill in a great circle. She was left alone, dancing in the midst. Horror of horrors, she couldn't stop! The other girls were laughing at her and pointing at her, and she couldn't stop. Round and round she danced in her pajamas, crying: "I can't!—I can't! —I'm tired—lemme go—*please!*" They came nearer and nearer, and suddenly they weren't the people she knew any more, but creatures gibbering at her. She shrieked wildly and leaped from the window, followed by the whole pack in full cry. On she raced through the air, towards the stars. She could feel hot breath on her neck—she was hot all over—she could scarcely breathe—she couldn't breathe—she was falling, falling, with the pack on top of her, down, down, down, screaming, terrified.

"It's all right! It's all right, dearie! Martha's got you."

"Martha!"

"Hush, hush, dearie! It's all right!"

"Oh, Martha, it was horrible! I was falling—oh! hold me."

"There, there, it was only a dream. Close your eyes and go to sleep again."

Martha sat on the edge of the bed, holding the little figure in her arms and rocking gently to and fro. She looked up into the pictured eyes of Janey Haverard and a smile seemed to pass between them. Kit had fallen asleep.

5. The Train

FOR LAURA HAVERARD to invite people to afternoon tea on a Saturday afternoon in June was unpardonable in Kit's eyes. Kit knew that she would have to appear, washed and brushed and tidied, and hand round the cakes. "You must show everybody that you *can* behave nicely occasionally," Laura would say. As if she had not enough to bother about already, with all the extra work for the Junior Medal.

"Remember to put on a clean frock this afternoon, Kit," said Laura at the close of dinner.

"Why on earth? What's happening?" asked Kit, bolting her last mouthful with considerably less relish than she had anticipated. It was jam roly, and she always liked to keep the sticky bit in the middle until the end.

"I want you to hand round for afternoon tea. Anna Maria Trimble and the Trimble girls are coming, and Miss Miggs and Mrs. Edgington and Mrs. Cray. And don't forget to make sure you have a clean pocket handkerchief. Last time you had a filthy one with a hole in it."

"Oh! Laura, I'd forgotten all about the beastly afternoon tea. Need I come?"

"Of course you must. Be sure to wash behind your ears

and clean your finger-nails. And mind you give your hair a good brush; it looks even worse than usual. You had better take out a clean pair of white socks; don't get them dirty, and then they'll do for Sunday."

Kit busied herself with clearing the table. It was no use protesting. But as soon as ever she was free, she raced round to Pony. Flight seemed to be the only resource. When they had collected Helen, they would take the tram to the terminus and then walk into the country. Nobody would mind much if Pony and Helen were late for tea. Kit would simply vanish and hope for the best. Martha would be sure to give her something when she returned home. Martha was a sport nowadays.

Laura did not think so. She expressed herself very strongly about Kit's disappearance, and told Martha she thought it was a pity she so often encouraged the child in her disobedience. Martha pursed her lips and said nothing, which annoyed Laura still more. Really, there were times when Martha seemed to be getting too difficult to deal with. But of course she was a treasure: there was no denying it. And the sponge cakes she had made for afternoon tea just melted in your mouth.

Out in the countryside beyond the terminus, the three were already deep in a pretending-game. They were playing French Revolution, and the howls of the mob could be heard from afar across the fields. Pony had rescued a whole family of aristocrats and was now paying on the scaffold for her gallantry. "It is a far, far better thing that I do than I have ever done," she chanted, and the mob howled again.

"Hurry up and kneel down!" urged the practical Helen. "There you are—plonk!—your head's off."

"All right! Now let's start again and rescue somebody

else."

"No you can't. You're dead. It's our turn," objected Kit.

"I'm not dead. I needn't be, anyhow. Let's pretend it's before I was dead. Oh, very well! we'll do something different. Let's practice for the sports."

Kit hated practicing for the sports, but it was not fair to say so. Pony had a very good chance of winning the Junior Cup. "All right, if you like," she agreed. "Let's do some jumping."

Helen produced some string from her pocket and they soon rigged up a jumping stand. She and Kit did pretty well for a while; then Kit fell out, and soon Pony was left to jump alone. She cleared the rope every time, landing neatly and coolly. "You can't miss the championship, Pony," declared Helen. "There's nobody to touch you. What about some catching?"

Pony was never without a grimy tennis ball concealed somewhere about her person. They stood some distance apart in the hot June sunshine and threw it from one to another. Pony and Helen did some quick work between them. After a while, Kit began to miss every time. "Do think what you're doing," grumbled Pony. "You're not looking at the ball at all."

"Sorry!" muttered Kit. "I was pretending French Revolution again."

"Well, don't!" said Pony. "Come on, we've been standing still long enough. Let's race."

They ran across the field first, then round it. Pony's long legs carried her far ahead of the others.

"Now, let's do a long-distance run," suggested Helen. "Let's run along the cart-track as far as the bridge over the railway."

It was a good deal farther than it looked. By the time they reached the bridge, they were all out of breath. Kit flopped down in the hedge and panted heavily. All of a sudden, she felt sick. She daren't tell the others. Somehow or other she must control herself.

"Dare you to walk along the parapet," cried Pony.

"Done!" snapped Helen.

She climbed up easily and walked stolidly from end to end of the bridge. The metals gleamed in the cutting down below. Far in the distance they could see the little station: the solitary signal was up. "Now, Pony, your turn!" said Helen as she jumped down.

Pony didn't worry. She stood poised for a moment at one end and then ran the whole way along. "Come on, Kit!" she cried.

Kit stood up a little dizzily. She had been feeling funny ever since the last race. But if she said so, they would think she was funking the parapet. The horrible thing was that she did funk it. Whatever happened, they simply mustn't find out.

She pulled herself up on to the parapet. It seemed ages before she could stand upright. She swayed a little as she walked.

"Look out, Kit!" warned Helen, and it was then that she heard it. A horrible rushing noise seemed to come from under her feet; a cloud of darkness swirled about her eyes. A train. She gasped wildly and felt something breaking against her chest.

"Kit!" shrieked Pony as she tottered, but it was Helen who pulled her down.

They fell in the cart-track together and for a long time she knew nothing at all. Then she saw the sky again, and the dark parapet just above her, and Pony and Helen sitting by her side with scared faces. "The train," she whispered. "It was the train."

"But there wasn't a train," said Pony.

"There was—I heard it—there must have been—I don't understand."

"Do you feel better now?" asked Helen abruptly. "Because if you do, I think we ought to take you home."

They dragged her up between them and set off soberly along the track. After a while, Kit pulled herself together. "It's all right, I can walk by myself now," she said. She felt bruised all over.

"I say," said Pony. "Need we tell them I dared you?"

"You're not going to tell anybody," exclaimed Kit. "Oh, please, you mustn't!"

"Of course we must," said Helen impatiently. "You were ill. You know you were."

"No, I wasn't really," lied Kit. "It was the train—I mean, it was me thinking there was a train—I mean—oh! can't you see I'll get into no end of a row? Laura'll be wild about my going without leave, and this would put the stopper on it. She'll never let me go with you again. I couldn't stand it. I couldn't, really."

Pony was obviously relenting. Helen stood firm. "We ought to tell," she insisted. "There must be something the matter, to make you go all funny like that."

"There isn't! There isn't!" wailed Kit. "And if you say there is, they'll make a fuss and keep me away from school. And I can't miss school, you know I can't, not with the Junior Medal coming on. *Please*, Helen."

"Be a sport, Helen!" urged Pony.

By the time they reached Thornley Mays, Kit seemed

to be quite well. After all, it would be a pity to upset her
again by making a fuss. They all sneaked in at the back
door, and Pony and Helen left her safely in the kitchen
with Martha.

"You're looking tired out, dearie," said she. "And what
a bruise you've got on your arm. Let me find something
to put on it before it gets any worse. You must have been
climbing some more of them trees. There, that'll soon take
the hurt out of it. Come and have your tea in here all cozy,
and then you can slip up to bed early. Miss Laura's gone
out with Mrs. Cray."

"Come on, Helen!" urged Pony with an expressive look,
and they ran off together. Everything seemed to be all
right.

The time for the Junior Medal examinations was drawing nearer and nearer. Even the Professor realized it at last.
He was surprised one evening to find her in his study, lying on the hearth with a book opened out before her. She
scrambled to her feet as he came in. "Sorry, Father!" she
said, shaking the tangled hair from her eyes. "It's chilly this
evening, and thou nearly always has a fire in here. I didn't
know thou was coming in so soon. I thought perhaps thou
wouldn't mind—"

"But of course I don't mind!" he interposed gently. "Surely
thou canst come in here whenever thou likes."

"Can I?" she asked, half-eager, half-surprised. "Can I
really, Father? Laura says I mustn't, because of disturbing
thee."

"Dear, dear!" He was puzzled at this and hesitated, looking
down at her and smiling nervously. He did not like to flout
authority. And of course Laura knew best. Laura was a dear
child: he could never have managed without her. "What art

thou reading?" he asked.

"Only homework. It's foul. I hate homework, and we get such a lot of it nowadays. Did thou have to do homework when thou was at school?"

"I suppose I did. I don't really remember much about it. I remember I had to study very hard to win a scholarship to Marston. I couldn't have gone there without it."

"And thou won it? Good for thee! Let's hope I win the Junior Medal."

"The Junior Medal? What is that?"

"It's an examination. It's only a week off now. Didn't thou know about it?"

"No, dear, I don't think I realized." The Professor looked vaguely at his daughter. "What does it mean?" he asked.

"Oh, you get a silver medal, and a scholarship, and a double remove, if you're lucky. It's no end of a swell affair. I wasn't going in for it at first, but then I thought I might as well have a try."

The Professor looked down thoughtfully at his small daughter. She did not seem to be pretty or musical, like Janey, nor had she Laura's practical gifts. Perhaps she would be clever and win scholarships. "Thou'rt growing up now," said he. "It's time thou learned to study."

Kit nodded. Prince Charlie and the clansmen seemed very far away; so did Carmen of the red rose. "I must go to bed now," said she. "Good-night, Father."

"Good-night, dear child," said he, and turned absently to his desk.

For the next few days, he watched Kit with interest. She was evidently working hard, slipping into her place at meal-times late, with inky fingers. "Why can't you remember to wash your hands, child?" Laura would say. He himself would gently remind her to say her Grace. She was apt to forget the customary silent communion of the Friends. She did not take long over her meals, he thought. He did not notice how poor an appetite she had. Only he thought she had grown very short-tempered of late. Perhaps she would be better when it was all over.

After the examinations came a short lull. Kit continued to be very cross and irritable, and Laura's patience was tried to breaking-point. Even Pony and Helen thought it best to leave her alone for a while. Only Martha persisted. She would pursue Kit with mugs of milk and slices of bread pudding, only to be rebuffed in the end. "Oh, leave me alone, Martha!" It was no use.

The results were to be announced publicly in the School Hall. Kit went down with a very white face. At home, her father moved restlessly about his study, unable to settle to anything. At last the telephone bell rang shrilly. "Miss Ferguson, Chesterham High School, speaking," said a calm, feminine voice. "Is that Professor Haverard?"

"Yes. What is it?"

"I'm just going up into the Hall to announce the Senior and Junior Medal results, and I thought I would like to ring up and congratulate you first."

"Congratulate me, Miss Ferguson? I'm afraid I don't quite understand you. What has happened?"

"Your daughter has won our Junior Medal, Professor. She is the youngest holder on record. I thought you would like to have the news first. Excuse me, my secretary says it's time we were in the Hall."

The Professor hurried in search of Laura with the good news. "Are you sure you heard correctly, Uncle?" she exclaimed. "Or was Miss Ferguson just telling you that Kit had done very well for her age? No? Well, this is really a splendid achievement. Kit's coming on at last, isn't she?"

The telephone bell sounded again. "I'll answer it," cried Laura and ran downstairs. The Professor followed more slowly. When he reached the hall, Laura had just banged down the receiver. Her face was set and white.

"Uncle, that was the High School ringing up again."

"Was it, dear? I hope there hasn't been a mistake."

"I'm to go in a taxi and bring Kit home."

"But—why—what's the matter?"

"They think it's her heart. Will thou telephone Doctor Cray?"

She slipped out like a ghost and, dazed, he went to the telephone.

6. *"The Old Order Changeth"*

KIT'S ILLNESS WAS her first experience of the delectable process of "spoiling." Former illnesses had been more or less ordinary affairs, taken in the general run of school epidemics and very efficiently nursed by Laura. Now, for the first time, she felt that she was really interesting. Moreover, she suspected that somehow or other she had managed thoroughly to scare the grown-ups. Laura had petted her in the most astonishing way and had wanted to move her into her own bedroom—an idea which Kit had resisted with all her might. Even Tom and Miles had written long letters from Marston, and Richard had sent a telegram. Of course, there were some things she did not like to remember. There was that moment in Hall, when the Headmistress had called her by name and she had risen to her feet before the assembled school. She could still hear the great roar of applause, and see the tiers of excited faces which had bobbed up and down so dizzily before her, until she had been swept away from them into nothingness. Of her awakening, she had no unpleasant memories. It was such a relief to be told to lie still and not to worry about anything.

There was worry enough and to spare to be found in the study downstairs, where the Professor paced to and fro across the worn carpet. Doctor Cray had tried to reassure him. "Come, come, Haverard, things aren't as bad as all that, though how we've managed to let the little maid get into such a state, the Lord alone knows. I blame myself for not watching her more closely, I do indeed."

"You?" repeated the Professor. "You blame yourself? Nonsense, Cray!—I only wish I could think so. But it seems so cruel that it should have happened now, just when the child was doing so well. We were beginning to have such hopes."

"That's just it," persisted the doctor. "We've all been in too much of a hurry. We must give the little maid time. Why, you'll not know her when she's been running wild for a bit. Hope away as much as you like. She'll surprise us all, some day."

The Professor allowed himself to be reassured. In his relief, he bought the entire stock of an itinerant flower-seller and presented it to Kit. Laura caught him in the act. "Oh, Uncle *dear!*" she exclaimed. "Now we shall have all the flower-sellers in Chesterham on the doorstep for weeks."

"But I thought thou liked flowers," marveled the Professor, and Laura, having kissed him and scolded him and straightened his tie, shut him up in the study again and paid a flying visit to the kitchen.

"Doctor Cray's very pleased with Kit this morning, Martha," said she. "Isn't that splendid? Poor little kid. To think we should have let things go on so long. But who would have thought that she was really ill?"

"Anyone would," came the grim rejoinder, "what had eyes in their heads."

Laura beat a hasty retreat. Things were none too easy for her. She was not allowed to forget.

Kit rallied more quickly than even Doctor Cray had dared to hope, but her convalescence proved to be disappointingly slow. At last Doctor Cray insisted that she should be sent away into the country. Laura protested at first that she did not know where to send her. Kit settled the whole question as soon as ever she heard of it. "I want to go to Manningleigh," said she.

"For heaven's sake, don't be so ridiculous, child!" exclaimed Laura. "Oh, I'm sorry, darling, but you wouldn't like it, really, you wouldn't! Whatever would you do in a sleepy little country town with three old ladies?"

"Of course I'd like it!" declared Kit. "I should love it. I should hate to go anywhere else."

"Mrs. Cray rang up this morning to say she knows of a very nice nurse at Roseville-on-Sea who takes in convalescent children," suggested Laura. "That would be much nicer for you, wouldn't it? The house is right on the shore and the sea-breezes would do you so much good. And it isn't too far away, so that I could come and spend a day with you sometimes. And you would have other children to play with."

"I don't want to go to Roseville-on-Sea," protested Kit. "It's a beastly place with a prom and a pier and shops and things. And I don't want to stay with a lot of children I don't know and be bossed about by a nurse. I want to go to Manningleigh."

"Well, stop fussing, or you'll run a temperature and not be able to go anywhere," said Laura irritably. It seemed an unfair advantage, thought Kit.

When Doctor Cray heard of it, through veiled hints from Martha, he took Laura aside. "Why shouldn't she go to Manningleigh?" he asked.

"It wouldn't be a bit suitable for the child," explained Laura. "How could the old ladies look after her? Miss Henrietta must be well over eighty, and I believe she's bed-ridden. I'm sure Miss Maria and Miss Priscilla must have enough on their hands without Kit, especially as she's such a difficult child. And then, Doctor, I'm afraid I've rather let Uncle drop out of touch with the Kitsons. He is so absent-minded, you know, and—well, I didn't want them to come bothering and interfering."

"I see," observed the Doctor quietly. "Have none of the boys been there since their mother died?"

"No," confessed Laura. "Miss Maria wanted me to take them for a visit, but somehow or other it never came off. Of course Aunt Janey took all three of them there at one time or another. Richard will remember perfectly."

"Supposing we consult him?" suggested the Doctor. Laura gratefully agreed. Surely her cousin could be relied upon to back her up. Richard, however, disappointed her. He was abroad with a reading party, but he wrote at once, both to Laura and the Professor, urging them to send Kit to Man-ningleigh if she wanted to go there. "I can't think how we've allowed ourselves to get out of touch like this!" he wrote. Laura bit her lip impatiently and decided that she had better eat her humble pie and write to Belceaster House.

An invitation for Kit arrived by return of post. Laura had an uneasy feeling that the whole affair was being taken out of her hands. Doctor Cray suggested that Kit should travel as far as London with his wife, who was attending commit-tees at Friends' House during the next week: it would be no trouble for her to see the child across London and put her on the train for Manningleigh at Waterloo.

"We'll do just whatever you think best, Doctor," agreed

Laura, in rather a flat, tired voice. There did not seem to be anything left for her to plan.

The day before Kit went away, Pony and Helen came for tea. "I'm going to cross London," she told them eagerly. "Isn't it exciting?"

"Isn't it just?" agreed Pony. "But of course, you won't see anything of London really. You ought to stay there some time and get to know it thoroughly, like we did."

"I wish I was going with you, Kit," said Helen wistfully. "Isn't Manningleigh near Belceaster? I once saw a picture of Belceaster Cathedral. It must be a wonderful place."

"Come on, let's do something!" suggested Pony, taking the lead again as usual. She had never been to Belceaster. And it would never do for Kit to get important about herself, what with her illness, and crossing London, and going to places that Pony had never heard of. "What about Lancelot and Elaine, for a change? I'll be Lancelot, and you can do Elaine, Kit, so that you'll be resting part of the time. Miss Haverard said we mustn't tire you before the journey."

Pony was beginning to attach a good deal of importance to what Laura said. Somebody had told her that Laura had been tennis champion at Heryot and captained the First Eleven Hockey. Obviously she was well worth knowing. Privately, Pony suspected that Kit had never really appreciated Laura. The fact that she had once shared Kit's opinion made her all the more anxious to win favor in her sight.

Kit shrugged her shoulders. She couldn't think why Pony had begun to "talk Laura" at her. And she hated being fussed, now that she was almost well again. "All right," she said grudgingly. "It's a long time since we've played it. But I don't know that I want to be Elaine very much, and what is there for Helen?"

"Of course you must be Elaine," insisted Pony. "It's the nicest part of all. Helen can be Lavaine and the Lord of Astolat—only I'll do him when Lancelot isn't there—and Gawaine and Guinevere and the dumb servant."

"Anything else?" asked Helen with a grin. "All right. Start off where you come to Astolat. Only what about Sir Torre?"

"Oh, miss him out!" exclaimed Pony impatiently, and without further delay they plunged into the story. It made rather a good play, except that there were too many love scenes in it. They hurried over them rather apologetically. Love scenes were always troublesome. The fighting bits were best.

At length Elaine, cruelly forsaken, proceeded to pine away. The action was becoming far too slow, thought Pony. "Buck up and get on to the dying part," she urged. Elaine did not seem to hear her. Nowadays, Kit had a way of losing herself in the play, which irritated Pony very much. She seemed to be taking their games more seriously than ever, whereas Pony was beginning to feel a little self-conscious about them. None of the other girls in her form played pretending-games. "Can't we skip a bit of this?" she suggested.

Kit lay back on the sofa, humming to herself. The words of Elaine's song from the *Idylls of the King* were running through her mind. Somehow or other, they were fitting themselves into a kind of tune as they went along. She began to sing tentatively; her voice was uneven and uncontrolled. The others scarcely listened. They were used to Kit's oddities by now, but they did wish she would hurry up, and Pony itched to sing it for her. The strange, disjointed thing ambled along, and Helen was just going to break in as Lavaine and put an end to it, when suddenly something seemed to break down in Kit. As if she had indeed been transformed into the lovelorn child of the story, she lost herself and sang:

> *Sweet love, that seems not made to fade away,*
> *Sweet death, that seems to make us loveless clay,*
> *I know not which is sweeter, no, not I.*
>
> *I fain would follow love, if that could be;*
> *I needs must follow death, who calls for me;*
> *Call and I follow, I follow! Let me die.*

Pony and Helen stared at her. They had never heard her sing like that before. Pony pulled herself together to break the spell.

"What's up with thee, Elaine?" she began, in the fatherly tones of the Lord of Astolat. "Art thinking of yonder knight?"

Kit said nothing. There were tears in her eyes.

"Look out!" whispered Helen. "She's going to cry. For goodness' sake let's play something else."

Pony nodded assent and plumped down on to the sofa. "Cheer up!" said she. "It was awfully nice, but don't let's do any more of it. The part where she goes down the river is a bit dull, isn't it? Let's try something else."

Kit shook herself slightly and sat up. "All right," she said gruffly. "Don't mind. Anything you like."

"Right-o!" said Pony, taking the situation in hand. "We'll do the last battle and you can be Arthur. You'd like that, wouldn't you? Helen can do Modred and Bedivere, and I'll be Lancelot."

"But he wasn't there," protested Helen.

"Can't help it," rejoined Pony. "And how do you

know, anyway?"

It was a relief to turn to action. *The Passing of Arthur* always made a good play, what with the fighting, and Excalibur, and one thing and another. There was a slight hitch over the Excalibur part, because Lancelot wanted to take Bedivere's place, but Helen persisted until she won her point, and Pony had to change into the Lady of the Lake for the time being instead, and produce an arm "clothed in white samite, mystic, wonderful." It was not the kind of part she liked to play, and she was annoyed with Helen for being so pig-headed. At last the sofa became the phantom barge of Avilion, and the broken king turned to look his last upon the bowed figures of his knights.

"The old order changeth, yielding place to new," Kit began.

Suddenly the door burst open. Laura looked in, cried "Sorry, dears!" and turned to flee.

Pony jumped up, blushing. "Oh, don't go, Miss Haverard!" she protested. "Why don't you come and play with us?"

"Why, you don't want me, do you?"

"Of course we do. We weren't doing anything really. You stay with us, and let's play a proper game."

"Very well. What shall it be? Consequences?"

"Yes, *please*, Miss Haverard."

"Right you are! Come along with me and hunt for pencils."

Kit still lay upon the sofa, bound for Avilion. Helen knelt beside her, a little twisted smile upon her face.

"The old order changeth, yielding place to new!" said she.

7. Belceaster House

MANNINGLEIGH WAS a very quiet place. That was the thing which most impressed Kit, the town sparrow from Chesterham. There were no trams to disturb the peace of the sedate High Street, and comparatively few motor cars. Shops and dwelling-houses flanked it side by side, the houses plain and dignified, and the shops, for the most part small and dark, with bow windows, lattice paned. At one end of it, near the little lane which led to the church, was an old-fashioned square called the Place, where her great-aunts lived. Very little traffic came their way. From the big garden behind Belceaster House you looked across Easingholme Farm and the almshouses to a low ridge of hills beyond. The little town might have been miles away.

Miss Maria and Miss Priscilla had lived in Manningleigh all their lives. Miss Maria was a tall, dignified old lady, with iron-grey hair and kind eyes, Miss Priscilla was a little frail thing, with snowy curls. To both of them, it seemed as if Janey had come home again at last.

Kit loved the quiet, uneventful life. She found no difficulty in filling up her time. There were plenty of books to read, and flowers to pick and errands to do for Aunt Maria, and endless wool to wind for Aunt Priscilla. Sometimes she even practiced on the lonely grand pianoforte in the drawing-room. It looked neglected there somehow, as if it was bored with having nobody to play on it. When she first asked permission, Aunt Priscilla looked a little doubtful, and cast an anxious, questioning glance at Aunt Maria. She, however, drew herself up severely. "Of course thou may practice, my dear," she said firmly. "*Nobody* can have the least objection." Kit wondered what all the fuss was about and began to feel a little shy.

She soon grew very fond of the old piano, with its worn ivories and mellow tone. The piano-stool had a round, embroidered top, worked by Great-grandmother Kitson long ago. It had a disconcerting habit of revolving suddenly in the middle of a piece, if Kit happened to get too excited. Perhaps Victorian ladies were more decorous. When she grew tired of practicing, she would wander round the room, exploring old cabinets full of family treasures, or examining the pictures which crowded the walls. The portraits and miniatures fascinated her. Aunt Priscilla had explained them to her many times. "That's Grandpa Kitson. We used to be rather afraid of him, but I'm sure he was a very good man. Only he used to growl at us. . . . There's Grandma in her Quaker bonnet. She was a very strict Friend. They say she never quite forgave dear Mamma for buying a piano. . . Grandma Shillitoe was rather *frivolous*. She used to wear curls, but I'm sure she couldn't help it. And she once bought a musical box—but it only played hymns." Before her own father's silhouette, Aunt Priscilla would pause with pride. "Thy great-grandfather was a most remarkable man," she would say. "He always used to blow out the candles with his nose."

There was an old-fashioned Victorian album of "select

pieces" among the pile of forgotten music. Kit discovered it one day and scrambled joyfully through the easy ones. There was a flamboyant march which pleased her hugely. She played it nearly every day, very loudly.

One day she was sitting at the piano, deep in a pretending-game. The town was besieged, the people were panic-stricken. Just as they were giving up hope, the march crashed out, and the sound of the martial music put courage into them again. A mighty throng moved towards the city gates, banners waving, swords in hands. The weary sentinel on the highest tower looked out once more across the plain and saw the helmets of the relieving army glistening in the sunlight. "Relief!" he cried. "Relief!"

The knights rode up the valley and the townsfolk leapt the wall, till a furious battle raged on every hand, to the thunder of the march and the growl of strident semi-quavers in the bass.

"Victory! Victory!" shouted Kit, as she jammed on the loud pedal and fumbled over the final chords. Suddenly she stopped, blushing furiously. She felt that someone was watching her. An old lady stood in the doorway, very tall and bent, leaning on an ebony staff. She wore a dress of deep crimson, with lace at throat and wrist. Her hair was thick and dark. Her smile was not kind. "Well, who are you?" she asked.

"I'm Kit—I'm Kit Haverard from Chesterham. I'm—my mother was Janey Kitson," stammered Kit.

"You play very badly." (Kit was crestfallen now, as well as frightened.) "You always put an accidental in the tenth bar. There isn't one. It's perfectly simple. Any fool could play it."

The old lady hobbled across the room, swept Kit off the

stool, and sat down at the piano. "Humph!" she said. "I can play it myself." Kit watched her eagerly. She played brilliantly, with a queer dash of bravado. "Well?" she demanded at the end.

"You—you play it very nicely—" began Kit tactfully.

"Humph! Nicely—everyone plays nicely. You play nicely. Susan plays nicely. Priscilla plays nicely. Nicely, indeed! What are you staring at me for?"

"I didn't mean—"

"Just so! Well, why do you do it? Is it my dress? Haven't you ever seen an old woman in a red dress before?"

The idea struck Kit for the first time. It interested her. Had she ever seen an old woman in a dress like that? "I don't think—" she began.

"Of course you don't think. Nobody thinks. I'm different. I please myself. I do what I like. I wear what I like. Maria and Priscilla can go to the devil in black if they choose."

Kit drew back a step or two. The old lady really looked very fierce. Nevertheless, she felt impelled to take up the cudgels in defense of her gentle great-aunts. "I don't think you ought to speak like that about Aunt Maria and Aunt Priscilla," she said, speaking rather loudly for fear of being interrupted. "I don't care who you are. They're good—ever so good—I won't let you." She took a step forward. Her heart was thumping furiously and her hands were clenched. "I won't let you," she repeated.

The old lady looked at her for a moment, dumbfounded, then reached for her staff and pulled herself to her feet. "Go away!" said she abruptly. "Go away, I tell you! Go away!"

Kit turned and fled. When she crept back to the drawing-room later, the old lady had gone. It seemed very hot and stuffy somehow. The smell of Aunt Priscilla's pot-pourri

nearly overpowered her. When Aunt Maria found her there and packed her off to bed, saying she looked poorly, she did not protest. Nor did she ask any questions. She was always chary of investigating too closely the private concerns of grown-ups.

Next day she spent the morning in bed. Later on, she took a deck-chair into the rose garden, where she lazed through the sunny afternoon, writing a letter to Pony in the intervals of shedding tears over *The Story of a Short Life*. Suddenly something made her look up. A boy was standing under the crimson ramblers, looking at her.

"Hullo!" said he. "You're Kit, aren't you? I'm Phil Kitson of Belceaster. I've biked over to see the great-aunts and they sent me out to find you. Charlie wanted to come, too, but he's got a punc. He always has, somehow. And the girls are at Grandad's with Mother. They'll get their hair off when they know I've seen you."

"Why?"

He grinned and sat down cross-legged on the ground beside her. "Oh, girls always want to be first, don't you think? And we've all been wondering what you would be like. Dad used to play with your mother here when they were kids. What's that you're reading? *The Story of a Short Life?* Rot! Why on earth do girls always like books about people who die young?"

"It's rather romantic, isn't it?" suggested Kit. There was a beautiful picture in the back of her mind of a little flower-decked coffin, and Laura and Miss Miggs and Miss Ferguson, all dressed in deep mourning. "Too late, too late, too late!" they wept in chorus. She began to compose a long epitaph for the tombstone.

"Romantic be blowed," laughed Philip. "Why not

enjoy life?"

Kit was beginning to feel at ease with him. "That's all very well," she said, "but what if other people don't let you?"

"That's rotten luck, of course," agreed Philip. "But it doesn't really matter, you know. Nothing does, if only you've got guts."

There was something familiar about this. "That's a funny way of putting it," said Kit slowly, "but it sounds a bit like what Doctor Cray said. He called it: 'feeling happy about things inside.' I suppose he meant if you can only keep your end up, you're all right, no matter what happens."

"That's it!" broke in Philip. "And if you can't, you're not living at all, really. If you're not yourself, you're just dead. Like old Aunt Henrietta."

"Aunt Henrietta?" At last Kit was on the scent. "Does she still live here?"

"Yes, of course. Didn't you know?"

"No. At least, I saw someone yesterday, in the drawing-room—"

"Oh, but you couldn't have seen her! It must have been somebody else. She never comes down."

"Why not?"

"There's something the matter with her back, I think. She says she can't manage the stairs, so she has a sort of flat on the top floor. But she went up there ages ago, when she quarreled with the aunts."

"Quarreled with the aunts? How could she? Why?"

"I don't know. But I think she quarreled with most of the family at one time or another, though I believe she was awfully fond of your grandfather. But Dad says, when Great-grandmother Kitson died, and he told them that the house was left between the three of them equally, she said:

'Very well, Charles, I shall take the top floor for my share, and you can all just leave me alone, from now on.' So she went up there and then, and that was that."

"But whatever was it all about?"

"Nobody knows. But Dad and Mother always say there are two sides to the question."

"I should think there must be. Anyhow, I shall go up and see her as soon as I can. I hope the aunts won't mind."

"Good Lord, no! But I shouldn't, if I were you. You'll only get your head bitten off."

Kit grinned. "Well, that'll be an interesting experience, anyhow," she said.

"Children! Children!" called a clear voice, and Aunt Maria came through the rose-covered trellis in search of them.

"There's something very *right* about Aunt Maria somehow," thought Kit, as they jumped to their feet. Involuntarily, she held up her face to be kissed. It was a rare gesture with her. The Haverard children were not encouraged to be demonstrative.

Tea was served in the drawing-room. Ordinarily, Kit had a substantial five o'clock tea, save on Sundays and special occasions. Philip's visit was evidently a special occasion. Kit loved the delicate charm of the tea table at Belceaster House. The cups were old family treasures, lightly sprayed in grey and gold, and poised daintily on slender bases. Aunt Maria would warm each one carefully, and then pour in the corn-colored Lapsang Souchong from the shallow Georgian teapot. A touch of cream from a Queen Anne cream jug, a lump of sugar from a wide, old-fashioned bowl, and the ceremony was complete. Never in her life would Kit take tea more pleasantly.

"And what were you two children talking about in the

rose garden?" enquired Aunt Maria, as she placed an almost invisible wafer of bread and butter in her saucer.

"Oh, lots of things!" replied Philip, trying not to swallow one of his aunt's famous shortbreads in one mouthful. "And by the way, Kit says she hasn't been up to see Aunt Henrietta yet. She wants to—don't you, Kit?"

Kit nodded shyly. She found it difficult to keep up with this unbounded self-confidence. Aunt Maria seemed to understand, for she smiled at her kindly and reached out to pat her hand. "I should like thee to visit her some day, dear," said she.

"Why not now?" suggested Philip. "I'll come, too."

The old lady shook her head and sighed. "Not today, dear boy!" she said. "My sister has not been well of late. Indeed, I have thought her ailing this last six months. I think she found the severe winter very trying."

"I'm sorry, Aunt Maria!" said the boy, blushing. "I didn't mean to barge in."

"Why, Philip, I am only too pleased thou shouldst take such thought for us. Only thou must understand that when she is poorly, she does not like to be visited. I have not seen her myself all this week."

The old lady paused and put down her teacup with a sigh. Philip changed the subject. "I say, Aunt Maria, your shortbreads are good. D'you mind how many I eat?"

"Just like his dear grandfather," twittered Aunt Priscilla. "Dost thou remember, Maria dear, how brother Charlie used to enjoy thy shortbreads? He once ate six at once, which was very shocking. I cannot tell how he could do it. But they are delicious shortbreads, are they not? My grandmother invented the recipe herself. She was a most remarkable woman."

"Well, I bet hers weren't any better than these," declared Philip, helping himself to another. "Hullo, what's that?" The harsh sound of a motor horn jarred on the quiet air. "Dash it, it's Mother and the girls!"

Aunt Maria raised a hand in deprecation of the language. Aunt Priscilla set down her teacup hurriedly and raised a lace-edged handkerchief to her lips. "Dear, dear! Dear, dear!" said she. "I still cannot get used to the idea of thy mother driving herself about. I cannot tell how she can do it. It really is not safe."

"You needn't worry, Aunt Priscilla, Mother can look after herself all right. But isn't it a sell when I thought I'd stolen a march on them? They must have decided to drop in on the way back from Grandad's."

"Thy cousin Brenda's father is Sir Hugh Cathcart, dear," explained Aunt Priscilla, in a hurried whisper to Kit. "He writes very wonderful music, I believe, but I have not heard any of it. Only it must be very good, because he was knighted for it. I do not care for modern music. The old is good enough for me. But I'm sure he's a most remarkable man."

There was a bustle in the hall. Philip sprang to the door and the newcomers burst in. The room seemed all at once to be full of people. Kit crouched in the background, happy to be left in peace. She studied Philip's sisters with interest. Emily, or "Milly," as they seemed to call her, was a year or so older than herself, strikingly lovely, with thick fair hair just touching her shoulders. Sheila was a stocky little thing, with a boy's crop and freckles. Their mother, "Cousin Brenda," was a big, handsome woman in an old tweed suit and brogues. Kit liked the look of her. She noticed that Philip was greeted with a careless: "Hullo, Phil, you here?" instead of an indignant: "Why didn't you tell me you were coming?"

"We've had a cup of tea, thank you," Cousin Brenda was saying in answer to Aunt Maria's enquiries. "We've only just dropped in. Now then, bairns, I want to talk to the aunts. Get along with you and let's have a bit of peace." She swept them all out of the room with a gesture, catching Kit on the way as she tried to slip past. "Come and shake hands, Kit. Do you like being kissed? I don't expect you do. Come and see us at Gramercie some day."

Kit ran on to join the others, and Philip linked her arm in his as they all swung off down the garden together. When they reached the wild part beyond the rose garden, they paused.

"What shall we do?" asked Milly.

"Let's tell stories," began Sheila hurriedly. "I started a new one today, and it's all about a family of fifteen children, and their names are Richard and Donald and Margaret and Monica and—"

Milly ignored her. "Let's sing," said she.

"Do you—can you sing, Emily?" began Kit shyly.

"Of course. And don't call me Emily. I hate it. You might as well call me 'Little Em'ly' and be done with it. And people say: 'Emily!—how nice! After your Aunt Emily, I suppose. She's such a *beautiful* person.' Bother Aunt Emily. You must call me Milly like everybody else, and that's bad enough. Come on, let's sing."

". . . and David and Daffodil," concluded Sheila imperturbably. "All right. I don't mind. What shall we sing?"

Philip did not await discussion. He sat, swinging back and forth on a fallen tree trunk, and began Schumann's *So wahr die Sonne scheinet.* Milly and Sheila joined in swiftly, Sheila supplying the alto. Kit had never heard anything quite like it before. She was longing to join in.

"Come on, what next?" urged Philip. "What do you sing at home, Kit?"

Kit blushed. "We don't," she confessed. "I'd give anything to sing like you do. I've learnt part-songs at school, of course, and my brothers know lots of funny ones—'Kafoozelem' and that sort of thing."

"Good old 'Kafoozelem'!" interrupted Philip. "Come on!"

They shrieked the chorus wildly and sang the verses in turn. Kit forgot herself in the general turmoil and joined in with the rest.

"I say, you can sing, you know," said Philip at the end. "Why didn't you say so?"

"Oh, she was only fishing!" put in Milly quickly, with a toss of her head.

Kit winced. She never seemed to be ready for this sort of thing. Philip came readily to the rescue—"Now then, Miss Smarty, speak for yourself—" and Sheila slipped a stubby hand into hers. "Don't be a piggy-wig, Milly," said she.

"After all, it would be funny if you couldn't sing," commented Philip. "Most of the Kitsons can. Some of them sing quite decently. My father, for instance, and your grandfather, and Great-aunt Henrietta, of course—"

"Great-aunt Henrietta," interrupted Milly. "You're potty. You mean Great-aunt Susan."

"No, I don't, clever," rejoined Philip. "I mean what I say. Aunt Susan sang prettily, just like anybody else—you, for instance. But Father says Great-aunt Henrietta had the most wonderful voice he's ever heard—and he knows what he's talking about. He only heard her once, when he was a little boy, and he's never forgotten it. She was in an awful paddy-whack. She hated being asked to sing."

"I wonder why?" mused Kit. "I should have thought it would have been fun."

"You'd better go and ask her," snapped Milly.

"Why not?" asked Kit, somewhat roused, and looking her pretty cousin straight in the face.

"You wouldn't go and see her?" asked Milly incredulously. "Not by yourself."

"Of course I would," declared Kit stoutly.

"You'd be scared."

"No, I shouldn't. I never heard such rot. I'll go and see her and find out what's the matter."

"You mean you'll go up there alone, without asking the aunts?"

"Yes, why not?"

"I dare you to."

"All right."

A voice called from the lawn above. "Children."

"Oh, come on!" urged Philip. "You just shut your face up, young Em'ly. Kit's all right. I'll bet on her."

Brother and sister tussled on the ground. "Em'ly" was the unforgivable insult. Honor satisfied, Milly rose and brushed the burrs off her skirt. Shaking the hair from her eyes, she flashed a sudden smile at Kit and seized her arm. Kit understood. Milly was like that. But in her innermost heart, she registered the dare.

8. *"Draw back the Curtains"*

IT WAS RATHER a stormy afternoon when Kit fulfilled her dare. Her aunts had gone to call upon the Miss Everitts next door, and had left her curled up with a book. Suddenly she realized that now or never was the time to visit Aunt Henrietta. She wanted to get it over. Secretly, she was beginning to funk it, and the longer she put it off, the worse it would be.

She knew the staircase which led up to Aunt Henrietta's rooms. She had seen Irwin, her attendant, going up and down many a time, carrying trays or armfuls of linen. It was an enclosed staircase, and a heavy door shut it off from the rest of the house. The stairs were uncarpeted. As she tiptoed up them cautiously, they seemed to creak with every step. At the top was a long corridor, with coconut matting, crimson-edged, and yellow, marbled walls. There was no one about. Irwin was doubtless indulging in a gossip over the teacups downstairs.

Kit pushed open door after door, very timidly. Some of the rooms were empty, and some were full of old-fashioned lumber. One, close at hand, was evidently Irwin's, neat and rather stuffy, with a big brass bedstead, and framed texts, and a stuffed bird, and a sewing machine. At the far end of the corridor were two doors with yellow glass handles: perhaps one of these would lead into Aunt Henrietta's room.

The farther door was slightly ajar, and guarded by a heavy plush portière. When she reached it, her heart beat fast. She knew that she had reached her goal. Her hand flew to her mouth, and she bit her finger thoughtfully. Then, pulling herself together, she knocked, and pushed the door wide open. She caught a glimpse of a darkened room, lit by flickering candles, a heaped-up fire, a green-eyed cat, a parrot in a gilded cage and, looming through the semi-darkness, a white-faced, menacing figure. A voice shrilled fiercely: "Who are you? I don't know. Nobody knows. Go away!"

Kit closed the door hurriedly, and the heavy portière flapped in her face. It smelt of moth-balls and candle grease. "She's a witch. I know she is," she muttered to herself, over and over again. Surely nobody could blame her if she ran away. But she couldn't bear to let Philip down—"Kit's all right. I'll bet on her." Nor could she face the mocking light of Milly's blue eyes with her dare unfulfilled.

"It can't have been true," she thought to herself. "I must have imagined it. Anyhow, it's no good funking it. I must go back."

She pulled herself together with an effort and turned the crystal door knob. The room was just as she had left it, mysterious in the candlelight. Her great-aunt was sitting in a big chair by the fire. She wore the same crimson dress, heavy with old lace, and about her shoulders was a shawl of emerald silk, with many-colored embroideries and a deep silken fringe. She did not look up, but stared fixedly into the fire, and on the other side of the hearth, the great black cat stared, too. Kit did not venture to speak. She stood, motionless, looking about the room. It was large and sparsely furnished, with windows on two sides, shrouded close in curtains which swept the floor. In one corner was a piano, and in the center stood a tall harp.

The first person to speak was the parrot. Clutching at the bars of his cage, he eyed her wickedly. "Who are you? I don't know? Nobody knows. Go away!" he screamed.

Kit jumped nervously, and then stood her ground. "I'm a Jacobite," she whispered to herself. "Jacobites don't run away. This is an adventure."

Suddenly the old lady turned her head. "Oh, it's you, is it?" said she. "Come in."

Slowly Kit advanced. "Shut the door," snapped a voice, and she obeyed. She did not know whether the command came from the great-aunt or the parrot, but she had a confused idea that it did not matter which in the long run. There was a little Chippendale armchair in the shadows, and this she drew up to the hearth. The great cat eyed her closely, and then stretched himself out at her feet, resting his chin on her toes. "He likes you," remarked Aunt Henrietta. "Cats are discerning creatures."

There was a long pause, during which the old lady looked Kit up and down. After all, the dark eyes did not seem quite so unfriendly. At last it seemed best to retaliate, although there did not seem to be much hope of staring Aunt Henrietta out of countenance. Solemnly she stared into the grim old face, until a question snapped like a pistol shot. "Well, what do they call you?"

"Kit."

"Eh?"

"Jane Kitson Haverard. Kit."

"Humph! I was very fond of your grandfather."

"Were you? I'm glad."

"You're not like him. He was a very handsome man."

Kit, utterly crushed, was silent.

"I don't know," continued the old lady. "There's something about you that reminds me of him. Janey didn't. She was a great deal too like her mother. Lydia was a niminy-piminy thing. Not good enough for Phil."

"How do you know?" asked Kit boldly. She had decided to try a new way of dealing with this terrifying relative. "I should think it was his own affair, wasn't it?"

"I was very fond of your grandfather," repeated Aunt Henrietta shortly. "Perhaps nobody would have been good enough for him."

She fell silent again, and Kit, awed by the unhappiness which brooded over the room, looked about her uneasily. Suddenly her attention was caught by a picture. It was lit up by two candles in heavy brass candlesticks, on a slender-legged table beneath. "May I look at that picture?" she asked timidly.

"Look at anything you like," was the brief reply.

It was an unfinished study of three child heads, framed in a thin gilt frame. The eldest was a blue-eyed girl with a sweet, pale face: her arm was about the shoulders of another little maid, dark-haired, black-browed, with a spray of wild briar on her breast. The youngest, a chubby, baby thing, was nestling up to her sisters, but the dark child stared straight out of the picture into the world. There was only the little hand on her shoulder to bind her into the group.

"Well, how do you like it?" asked Aunt Henrietta abruptly.

"Ever so much," breathed Kit.

"Humph! Well, take a good look at it. You may not see it again. I shall pitch it into the fire, one of these days."

"Oh, no! No! You couldn't do that."

"Yes, I shall. What else can I do with the things I care about? Who'll want them when I'm gone? I'm not leaving a lot of stuff for people to haggle over. They've haggled enough. They've haggled the life out of me, between them. And that picture—means something. I shan't let them have it. Unless—unless you want it. Phil's grandchild. I shouldn't mind that. Would you like to have it some day? Very well."

She hobbled across to a little desk, candle-lit, and taking a silver-mounted pen from her belt, scrawled across a half-sheet of notepaper in a spidery hand: "The painting of Sophia, Susan and myself as children is to go to my great-niece, Jane Kitson Haverard."

"Who painted it?" asked Kit.

Aunt Henrietta shook her head and, crossing the room with some difficulty, stood beneath the picture with her hand on Kit's shoulder. "We never knew," said she. "He was a foreigner, and very famous in his own country, I believe. He was painting in the big Easingholme meadow beyond our paddock, and he saw us leaning over the gate. Afterwards, he sent this to Papa. There was no name with it."

"What were you doing?"

The old lady laughed bitterly. "Making plans," she said.

"About all the things you were going to do?" Kit sympathized with plan-makers. She made so many herself. Her aunt nodded, and made her way back to the fireside again, leaning heavily. She let herself down into the big chair and sat there, staring into the fire.

"Making plans," said she. "Susan said: 'I want to be pretty, and have a nice husband and some dear little babies.' She got there all right. And Sophia said: 'I'm sure I don't know.

I'm too happy to make plans. But I should like to have much to do, and always plenty of people to love and care for, and never to harm anybody or anything, and not to grow tired at last.' Well, she got there too, you know. But things were never the same after she died."

"And you? What was your plan?"

The old lady's expression changed in a flash. "What are you talking about?" she screamed. "Hold your tongue, child. Go away!" In the gleaming cage behind her, the parrot fought the bars, squawking wildly: "Who are you? I don't know. Nobody knows. Go away!"

Kit did not go. Stubbornly she stood her ground, sitting squarely in the little Chippendale chair with her feet on the fender. She was not afraid of Aunt Henrietta any more. She was only intensely curious.

"I'm always making plans," said she. "Laura says I make too many. She says I ought to pay more attention to my work and leave other things alone. And I did try, you know, only it seems it was all a mistake. So grown-ups can't always be right, can they? But when I asked Laura about it, she said they always knew best in the long run, and I mustn't go mooning round getting ideas into my head."

"If you can't live your own life, you're not *you* at all," snapped the old lady suddenly.

Kit went on thoughtfully. "That's just what Philip said. If you're not *you*, you're not alive really. You're just dead. It seems a bit rotten, doesn't it? I wonder if you ever get a chance to start again."

Aunt Henrietta did not speak. Kit saw to her surprise that there were tears in her eyes. She thought she had better change the subject, and racked her brains for a suitable beginning. The old lady stayed her with a gesture.

"I'm tired," she said simply. "I think I'll go to bed. Perhaps you had better run away before I ring for Irwin."

Kit slid to her feet. "I hope I haven't tired you, Aunt Henrietta," said she.

"No, no, it's nothing. It will soon pass off. But remember this, child: the tragedies of this world are the broken dreams of youth. There, get along with you. You won't understand."

Kit made for the door, then turned back impulsively and dropped a kiss on the wrinkled forehead. Slowly and thoughtfully, she made her way downstairs.

Late that night, she was still thinking about her secret visit. She tossed about restlessly and wondered why she could not go to sleep. The storm raged fitfully without, and the wind wailed mournfully round the old house, tearing at the sturdy window-frames and slamming doors in the lonely corridors. She was just a little afraid.

She could not remember falling asleep, but somehow or other she had turned into little Sophia Kitson. She was wandering up and down the house in a crinoline and lace trousers. A host of childish voices called her, begging for new games and stories, and older voices clamored, too—"Sophia, dear, come and help Mamma." "Child, child. Where are my spectacles?" She trotted about busily, until at last there came a fresh voice: "Sophia! Sophia!" and then again: "Sophia! Sophia!" and again and again, wailing down the wind. The light faded, and a storm broke out, and up and down the house she wandered, seeking the phantom voice. "Wait, I am coming," she called, and fainter and fainter came the cry: "Sophia! Sophia!" The storm raged more fiercely, and the landing window yawned before her. Out she went, and away on the wings of the wind across the stars—"I am coming—I am coming"—till she reached the mountains of the moon. There, on the edge of a vast crater, she paused, and up from the depths came the dying voice: "Sophia! Sophia!" Down she leaped with the answer on her lips, there was a crash and a peal of thunder, she was sitting up in bed crying, and the bedroom door had blown open.

She did not wait to think. She was still living in her dream. Swiftly she pulled on her dressing-gown and, thrusting her feet into her slippers, pattered towards the door. Up the back-stairs she fled, past the closed door behind which Irwin slept soundly, and down the dim corridor to the big, end room. There was nobody there. She was just beginning to feel frightened when the black cat brushed against her knee. She bent down automatically to rub his ears, and felt the great ruff on his neck bristling. A faint voice came from the adjoining room. "Sophia! Sophia!"

She tucked the cat under her arm. He was rather comforting and he reminded her of Jemima. Then she pushed open the door and stepped across the threshold. In the wavering candlelight, she saw her great-aunt in a big four-poster bed, raised up on the pillows. The old eyes were turned towards her. "I thought thou wert never coming!" said Aunt Henrietta. "I was frightened in the storm."

"It's all right!" said Kit reassuringly. She wondered why a grown-up should be scared in a storm, and why Aunt Henrietta did not seem to know who she was. She had never heard her use the Quaker "plain tongue" before.

"Thou'lt stay with me, Sophia?" came the weak, pleading voice.

"Of course I will. You'd better try to go to sleep again." Kit felt immensely grown up—almost like Laura.

The old lady stared straight into the shadows. "Dost thou

remember the other day," she began, "when we were leaning over the gate and the stranger was painting in the meadow? Didst thou mean what thou said in thy plan?"

"I—I don't quite understand what you're talking about," stammered Kit nervously.

"That thou wanted much to do, and plenty of people to love and care for, and not to grow tired at last: didst thou mean it, Sophia?"

"I'm sure Sophia meant it," replied Kit, feeling her way. She could not understand this at all. Perhaps Aunt Henrietta had been dreaming about the past and could not wake up properly.

"It wouldn't be enough for me, Sophia. I'm not like thee. I never shall be like thee. Thou'rt the sort of daughter Papa and Mamma want. So is Susan. But I'm different. Oh, I was born in the wrong place, dear, and I shall never get out."

Kit leaned over the bed and took the old lady's hand. "But you will, really and truly!" she said.

"No, I shan't. What's the good of wanting to make music when Papa won't hear anything but hymns? What's the good of Art if it's the work of the Devil? What's the good of making plans if they never come true?"

"They will come true, they will," urged Kit. She did not know why.

"Art thou sure?"

"Yes."

"Then draw back the curtains, Sophie dear. Let in the light."

Kit slipped across the room and, pulling back the heavy curtains, drew up the blind. The storm had passed over, and the full moon rode gallantly over the clouds. The white light poured into the room and fell full upon the bed. She returned to her place and took up the frail hand again.

"Thou'lt stay with me till I go to sleep?" urged the tired voice.

"All right." Kit would have liked to pop in beside her, but she hesitated to suggest it. It was rather cold.

The old lady opened her eyes again and began to mutter quietly to herself. *"Du holde Kunst,"* she whispered, *"in wieviel grauen Stunden."* Kit could not understand the words. She was getting very sleepy. Suddenly Aunt Henrietta repeated very slowly: *"Ich danke dir!"* and then again, more faintly: *"Ich danke dir!"* She looked up into Kit's face and sighed. "Sophia!" she whispered. "Sophia dear. Look at the light!"

Aunt Henrietta lay sleeping very quietly, and Kit sat on at her side, half-asleep. At last she stirred and shook herself. She was nearly frozen. Her aunt was quite peaceful now. Surely she might leave her. She bent over her and smoothed the tumbled sheet. The hand which had lain in hers was cold as ice. Gently she slipped it beneath the blankets and tip-toed quietly out of the room. Aunt Henrietta did not wake.

9. Gramercie

NEXT MORNING, "Cousin Charles" came over from Belceaster in a battered old Cromwell and spent some time with the aunts. Afterwards, he took Kit back with him to Gramercie. Aunt Maria and Aunt Priscilla kissed her hurriedly and bundled her into the car, as if they were afraid lest she should ask questions. They seemed to be distressed over something, and the household had lost its atmosphere of peace. Kit could not help overhearing Aunt Maria whisper to Cousin Charles as they set off: "Tell dear Brenda that the child does not know. I think it would be better to say nothing yet. Let her enjoy herself with her little cousins. Perhaps—later on—but it is all so very distressing, Charles dear."

Kit loyally refrained from seeking an explanation, and Cousin Charles did not seem disposed to offer one. Kit liked the look of him. He was big and burly and good-looking, with blue eyes set in a sunburnt face. "You're Philip and Milly and Sheila's father, aren't you?" she asked.

"Yes. They came over the other day, didn't they? They've been yammering at me to bring you to Gramercie ever since. I hope you'll like it. Now, look over there, between those trees, and you'll see the Cathedral towers."

Kit had not seen anything quite so beautiful before. She leaned back in her seat and watched the towers grow clearer and lovelier as they drove into the outskirts of Belceaster.

She was a little surprised when Cousin Charles stopped at the entrance to a cobbled alley. In Chesterham, people do not live down cobbled alleys if they can help it. "Hop out!" commanded Cousin Charles. She obeyed wonderingly. On her right hand was a high brick wall, with trees overhanging it at intervals: on her left was a long, rambling stone house, with tiny mullioned windows set high up, and, farther down the alley, a heavily molded archway over a massive oak door. It looked forbidding at first, but when she reached the door, she found it flung open to reveal a long, flagged passage-way, paneled on either hand, and beyond, through another door, a glory of color in an old-world garden.

Milly and Sheila came running to meet her. "Mind you look after her," called Cousin Charles, as they led her up the winding staircase to her room.

"I say, Milly, I did it," said Kit, as she put down her case. "I went to see Great-aunt Henrietta!"

"What on earth for?" rejoined Milly.

"But you dared me to," protested Kit.

"Did I? How silly of me. I'd forgotten all about it," said Milly carelessly. "How did you get on?"

Kit stiffened. If that was how Milly was going to take it, she wouldn't tell her anything. "Oh—it was all right," she said.

"I think it was jolly plucky of you," declared Sheila comfortingly. "Do tell us what happened."

But Kit did not want to talk about Aunt Henrietta, not while Milly was in one of her moods. Milly would only make fun of her. And somehow or other, Kit could not bear to think of anybody making fun of Great-aunt Henrietta.

"We didn't do anything special," she admitted grudgingly. "We just talked. And there was a big black cat, and a parrot in a cage—"

"Oh, I know all about *that*!" interrupted Milly. " 'Who are you? I don't know. Nobody knows. Go away!' Come on, don't let's bother about Aunt Henrietta any more. She's dead, anyhow."

Kit paused as she followed her cousins out of the room. That was what Philip had said in the rose garden. "If you're not yourself, you're just dead. Like old Aunt Henrietta." And it wasn't true, only she did not feel like arguing the point just then. Milly would never understand.

Kit fell in love with Gramercie at first sight. Milly did most of the showing round. Sheila, as usual, was making up a story. She loitered behind the others, muttering to herself—"Ha, ha, Roderick! thou shalt not escape. Where is the buried treasure?". . . "He had six brothers, and their names were Richard and Randolph and Rupert and Olaf and Cuthbert and Jabez." Nobody paid any attention to her.

It was not until they were all three perched on the deep window ledge in the girls' room that Kit began to ask questions. "Why do you call it Gramercie?" said she.

"Because of the old abbey which used to be here," explained Milly. "It was founded by a wicked baron called Fulk de Courteville. He thought his only daughter, Idonea, had been drowned at sea on her way home from a pilgrimage. The ship was wrecked on the rock of St. Merlyon near the Cornish coast. When Idonea turned up alive, he said: "Gramercie to Our Lady and St. Merlyon, and may God be merciful to me, a sinner." They put those words on his tombstone when he died, and that's where the Gramercie comes in."

"But this house isn't big enough for an abbey," objected Kit.

"It's only a bit of one, silly. The church of St. Merlyon, across the road, was part of it, too, and the public garden was the cloister. Most of the other buildings have gone, and this nearly went, too. It was split up into tenements and got into such a mess that they were going to pull it down when Great-great-uncle Shillitoe Kitson bought it for a song and came to live here with his daughter, Isabella."

"In tenements?"

"Of course not, silly. He restored the whole place and made it like it is now."

"It must have been like making it all come alive again," said Kit. "It's lovely to think we brought Gramercie back to life."

"We? I like that," snapped Milly. "Who are you, anyhow? You're not one of us."

"I am," rejoined Kit stoutly. "I'm every bit as much a Kitson as you are, so there."

"So she is," laughed Cousin Brenda from the doorway. "And more than I am, by right. I only had the good sense to marry one of them. Come along, all of you, it's dinner-time."

Sheila scrambled hurriedly off the window seat. "Been writing, Mother?" she asked. An ink-stained forefinger was held up by way of reply. "So've I. It's all about a boy called Roderick, and he had six brothers, and they were called Richard and Randolph and Rupert and Olaf and Cuthbert and Jabez. May I have some more manuscript paper, please?"

"Take as much as you want. There's a pile on my desk."

"And do you mix up the illustrations with the writing, or do you do them separately?"

"Well, the publishers don't seem to like my illustrations, so I don't send them any. But if I were you, I'd do them on drawing paper and then pin them into the proper places afterwards. Only don't let's bother about it now, because we're late for dinner, and I don't know whether your hands want washing, but mine do."

They all raced off together, leaping the unexpected steps which appeared in every dark passage, and bursting into the white-tiled bathroom with a shout. Milly threw the soap at Kit and everything was all right again. People did not fuss at Gramercie. Downstairs, they found Charlie and Philip waiting for them. Charlie was a tall, good-natured lad, very like his father, and a little like Tom, Kit thought.

After dinner, Philip took charge of her. "You needn't worry about Kit, Mother," said he. "She's coming with me."

The matter was settled without further discussion. Kit noticed an entire absence of the familiar battery of questions—"Where are you going?"—"What are you going to do?"—"What time will you be back?" Cousin Brenda seemed to manage without them.

"I may as well show you Belceaster," he suggested, as they closed the heavy door behind them. "Charlie's going over to Grandad's, to try out his new concerto, and we don't want to be bothered with the girls."

They left the cobbled alley and, turning to the right, walked down the road, past St. Merlyon's church, to the river and the comely arch of the bridge. On the opposite bank, the white Cathedral rose from its green knoll: Kit wished that Helen could have been with her to see it, too. "May we go inside it?" she asked.

"Of course," Philip assured her. "I really wanted to show you Kitsons, but we can have a look at the Cathedral first, if you like."

"What's Kitsons?" asked Kit, as Philip leaned over the parapet and fumbled in his pockets to find something to shy at a dead branch which was floating downstream.

"The business, of course," replied Philip. "Surely you know about that? Your grandfather used to be in it, and so was mine. Dad and Uncle Robert run it now."

"I remember," rejoined Kit. "Martha told me. Grocers and tea merchants, weren't they? But you're not going to be a grocer and tea merchant, are you?"

"I don't see why not," said Philip, "but I'd rather be a surgeon. Charlie can carry on with the tea merchanting. He'll be jolly good at it."

"But I thought he was the musical one," protested Kit. "Didn't he say he was going over to your grandfather's to try out his new concerto?"

"Well, what of it?" said Philip. "Why shouldn't a merchant be a good musician? Charlie's jolly keen on the business, but he's not going to sell his soul for it. You folk seem to have got hold of some jolly rum ideas about music, one way and another."

"I think we have," agreed Kit meekly. She wondered what Laura would have said.

They crossed the bridge and went through a maze of narrow streets flanked by old gabled houses, till they reached the broad sweep of Deanery Row and the West Front of the Cathedral. Philip pushed open the great door in the south aisle and stood aside to let Kit pass. They stepped softly about the old building, speaking very little. When they came to the de Courteville tombs, Philip stopped to show her the great de Courteville window above them, with its legends of the crusades. Kit thought he looked like a crusader himself. Some day, she would love to play pretending-games with him, only perhaps he was too old for them and would laugh at her. The sunlight slanted through the old window and threw a pattern of gold and crimson and emerald about their feet. The old verger watched them and thought they were an interesting pair. He wondered why they were so silent. Perhaps they hardly knew themselves.

A large party of tourists collected in the crossing and began to chatter. Kit shuddered slightly. The spell was broken. "How can they do it, Philip?" she exclaimed. "It's as if they were talking in Meeting."

Philip took her arm. "Come on, let's get out," he said. "It's time we hurried up. Dad's coming home early today."

They went home by the High Street. On the way they passed a fine Georgian house, with shops on either hand. "That's Kitsons," said Philip, pulling up suddenly.

The satellite shops were modern, but the main entrance was still a narrow door beneath a gracious fanlight, with pot-bellied latticed windows at each side. The windows exhibited tea-chests and spices: above the door was the inconspicuous sign of "Charles Kitson & Sons, Grocers and Tea Merchants."

"That's where we all come from," continued Philip. "That's where old Shillitoe lived before he bought Gramercie, and Grandpa for a time, and his grandfather, old Charles Kitson, long ago."

"Who lives there now?"

"Nobody. It's the biggest restaurant in Belceaster. Dad set that ball rolling when he was a youngster, and didn't he just catch it."

"Why?"

"Oh, Grandpa didn't like new-fangled ideas. He got still more of a shock when they opened the cafe in Belmouth."

Kit linked her arm with his and they strolled on together. "Belmouth? That's where my grandfather lived, isn't it?" she asked. "My grandfather, Philip Kitson."

"Yes. That branch was started for him. After he died, nobody did much with it. But when Uncle Robert got hold of it, he fairly made things hum. He runs the smartest cafe in Belmouth, and that's saying a good deal. When he put in a dance-floor, we thought Grandpa would have a fit."

"But you don't have dancing at the old place here?"

"No. That's different. Belmouth's a flashy sort of place."

They reached the bridge again and hung over the parapet, looking down into the water. "Different places want different things, somehow." commented Kit. "I shouldn't like dancing at Kitsons, but it would be all right in Belmouth, I suppose."

Philip pursued his own train of thought, swinging away from the parapet as he spoke and walking on slowly. "It's the same with people," he said. "You know at once when you've got the right person with the right outside. Not just a sham. Dad and Mother, for instance."

Kit turned to look back at the white towers of the Cathedral rising grandly above the river, and then hurried after him. "People who are themselves," said she. "That's people who've found the real me, I suppose. But lots of folk don't seem to get a proper chance, Philip. I think that's what's the matter with Great-aunt Henrietta. She said she was born in the wrong place and could never get out. Only before she went to sleep, she seemed quite happy again, but then she began talking in some sort of foreign language and I

couldn't understand. I wanted to go and see her again this morning and ask her what she meant, but your father was waiting, and it would have taken so long to explain it all to the aunts."

"Do you mean to say they haven't told you?" asked Philip.

They were nearing Gramercie now. Cousin Charles's rapid footsteps were catching them up as they reached St. Merlyon's Church. He was hurrying home to join the family for tea.

"What haven't they told me?" asked Kit, but she knew the answer.

"Great-aunt Henrietta died in her sleep last night," said Philip. "The aunts sent for Dad early this morning. He said she looked very peaceful, as if she had found herself."

"Perhaps she had," suggested Kit.

Cousin Charles caught them up, and they fell in on either side of him. He looked at them enquiringly. Something was obviously the matter.

"Nobody told Kit anything about it," explained Philip.

"The aunts thought you would be upset," said Cousin Charles. "They are terribly upset themselves, poor dears. But you mustn't take it that way, Kit. It's far better as it is."

"Kit saw her only last night," persisted Philip.

"I thought so," said Cousin Charles, "when I found the paper on her desk. Can you tell me just how it all happened, Kit?"

The little story was quickly told.

"So she fell asleep, did she?" asked Cousin Charles at the close.

"Yes," replied Kit. "So I thought I could go back to bed again. I was getting sleepy, too. But I covered up her hands before I went. They were so cold."

"Thank you, Kit," said Cousin Charles. They stood in the doorway of Gramercie, and the fragrance of the garden met them in the heat of the afternoon sunshine. "Henrietta Kitson might have been a great singer and a happy woman," said he, "but it was willed otherwise. Thank God times have changed. But remember, when you talk about women's freedom, that women like your Great-aunt Henrietta have paid a heavy price."

He turned to go in, but Kit pulled at his coat sleeve. "Please, Cousin Charles, what did she mean at the end?" she asked. "She said something like *'ich danke dir,'* over and over again."

"Did she?—hm!—*'ich danke dir'*—'I thank thee'— you'll hear that again some day, Kit, when you listen to Schubert's song, *An die Musik*. It's one of the loveliest songs ever written. I once heard Henrietta sing it. But I don't know what she had to be thankful for."

"Didn't you—didn't you say she looked as if she had found herself?" said Kit.

10. *"Du holde Kunst"*

KIT'S LAST EVENING at Gramercie threatened to be a disappointment. They had planned it out almost to the last moment, a walk along the riverside, a special supper, and music until bedtime. The evening was generally the best part of the day at Gramercie. One by one the family would drift in. Charlie would sit down at the Bechstein: he was a keen pianist, and Kit loved to hear him play. Secretly, she infinitely preferred him to Miss Miggs. Philip would take out his fiddle, and Milly would perch herself on the arm of the nearest chair. She had the greatest objection to sitting in anything for long. Wild things mistrust a cage. Cousin Brenda would establish herself by the fire with a basket of mending, and Cousin Charles would settle down in his favorite armchair with a book and a pipe. "Come on, Father, we want a baritone," they would cry, and he would lay his book aside and join in. Sheila, weaving one of her innumerable romances, would take refuge at her mother's feet until bedtime. Kit had been hoping that her last evening would be just like the others, only even better, if that were possible.

They came back from their walk to find Cousin Brenda waiting for them at the door. "Is that you, bairns? Oh, thank goodness! You must all run up and change quickly. Grandad has sent Papa Andreas over with a pupil. I do hope the supper will go round. However, it's an ill wind that blows nobody any good. We ought to have some good music."

They raced upstairs to an accompaniment of hurried instructions. "There's a clean shirt in your second drawer, Phil.—Use a bit of pumice stone for those ink-stains, Sheila bird.—Sorry, all of you! I'm afraid it will have to be tongue and chicken instead of chicken and tongue. Play up, won't you?"

Kit reached her bedroom with a bound and began to delve in the chaos of the bow-fronted chest of drawers. One by one she laid her things out on the bed, Liberty silk frock, white undies, yellow beads, silk socks and sandals. Philip poked his head round the door. "What a go!" said he. "I've brought you a jug of hot water. Milly and Sheila are still in the bathroom. I think they must be drowning each other." He put down the ewer and turned to go.

"I say, Phil, stop a minute. Who's Papa Andreas?" asked Kit.

"A friend of Grandad's. You'll like him no end."

"Shall I?"

"Of course you will. What are you worrying about, silly? Is that enough hot water, or shall I bring some more?"

"Oh, no, thanks. It's lots. I'm not going to drown myself. I say, Phil."

"Yes?"

"You've got an awful tide-line."

"Thank you, miss. Shall I wear a collar or shall I wash my neck? Bye-bye! Don't forget to wash behind your ears."

Kit hurled her sponge at his retreating figure and then set to work. Swiftly she pulled off her linen frock and knickers.

"It's a shame!" she whispered to herself. " 'Good music.' That means a 'musical evening.' And on my last evening, too, of all the rotten luck."

For years, musical evenings at Thornley Mays had been an enigma to Kit. Even with her limited experience, they presented a spectacle of unmitigated boredom. Her mind flew back to the last one she had endured before her illness—how she had hated it.

"I think I had better have a musical evening on Thursday week," Laura had said. "I've not had the Campions here for ages, and then there are the Selligers and the Fenwicks and the Trimble girls. They might bring Anna Maria with them. She would enjoy it so, poor old soul. And Mrs. Cray must come, of course, and Miss Miggs to accompany. You can stay up if you like, Kit, for a great treat."

Kit said "All right," as gloomily as she dared, thereby bringing down the retort upon her head: "If you're not musical, you ought to be. And you might at least try to appreciate people who are."

As the time drew near, the whole routine of the house was overthrown. The Professor was hounded out of his study and sent upstairs to change, protesting helplessly. "But I thought thou said I needn't dress."

"Of course not, Uncle. But you can't possibly sit in the drawing-room in those old trousers. And do put on a clean collar. I've left one out ready."

When the guests arrived, Kit was sitting in a corner of the drawing-room, painfully tidy, her face shiny with soap. A pleasant babble of small talk arose, and then the Professor buttonholed Garth Fenwick to ask after his father. "Pity Laura didn't invite him," he said—old Joseph Garth Fenwick notoriously disapproved of music—"I wanted to discuss his article in the *Friends Commentary*."

"Did you, sir?" The young man's face lit up with interest. "I told Pater you'd have something to say about it. Now, there's one thing I want to ask you—"

"Very good! Very good! Let's come through into the other room."

The Professor set off joyfully for the study with his willing visitor in tow, only to be waylaid by Laura. "Now then, Uncle, you mustn't run away with Garth Fenwick. The coffee is just ready, and then we are going to have some nice music."

Kit bestirred herself to hand round. There was nothing particularly thrilling to eat: she would have swapped the lot for a good thick slice of bread pudding any day. After the refreshments came an awkward pause, until at last Laura smiled brightly at Miss Miggs and said: "Perhaps you would set the ball rolling, Miss Miggs. We should all love to hear you play."

Miss Miggs coughed and smiled, and very deliberately took off her rings and arranged them in a neat little pile on the pianoforte. "I'm sure, Miss Haverard, you're far too kind," she said. "And I really don't know what to play; I'm so out of practice. However, perhaps I can remember a little piece."

She waited until everyone was silent, which took rather a long time. She even had to give a little disapproving "hem!" before people would be quiet. Kit felt hot all over. However, in the end, she obligingly set the ball rolling, and afterwards it rolled on and on, each in turn giving it the necessary push. Laura, from her little straight-backed chair, superintended the pushing. "Thank you so much, Miss Miggs. That was delightful. Now, Mr. Campion, I do hope you've remembered to bring some songs."

Mr. Campion, a dark, square man with a blue chin,

invariably started with "On the road to Mandalay." Kit listened, stupefied, and wondered if it didn't really hurt him to go all purple in the face like that. Everyone clapped at the end, and then Mr. Campion bowed and coughed, and took up another song. Kit wondered whether it would be "Kabul River," or "Uncle Tom Cobbleigh." Mr. Campion did not know many songs.

Afterwards it was Daisy Trimble's turn. She giggled shyly and produced the roll of music upon which she had been sitting all the evening. Her voice wobbled all the time she was singing, and Anna Maria evidently found it very affecting. Nobody could ever hear the words of her songs, but they were generally understood to be religious. It wasn't safe to clap Daisy overmuch. She never knew when to stop.

Kit heaved a sigh of relief when Laura asked Jocelyn Fenwick to play. Garth brought in the violin, and his wife opened the case swiftly with slim, capable hands. "Garth will accompany me," she said.

"Oh, but I'm sure Miss Miggs—"

"No thanks. I always play with Garth."

The performance was greeted with the usual perfunctory applause, but for once Kit did not join in. Afterwards she crept up to Jocelyn Fenwick and whispered in her ear. "Aren't you going to play again?"

"I don't think so. Why?"

"I want you to. You're different. Do play again, *please*."

Somebody addressed Garth jocularly. "Didn't know you played the piano. Give us a piece."

"Sorry!" replied Garth briefly. "I don't play solos."

Afterwards everybody agreed that the Fenwicks were delightful people, but it was a pity they were inclined to be a little superior.

At last the Selligers' turn came. Little Mr. Selliger, standing on one leg beside the piano and delicately poising his pince-nez askew upon his nose, sang very anxiously in a reedy tenor. Kit dared not look at him too much. He was just like a young cockerel trying to crow. Stout Mrs. Selliger sang a solo, too, in her heavy contralto voice. She sang about something stirring in the forest which turned out to be a bird, and Kit considered privately that it sounded much more like an elephant. They ended with a duet. Miss Miggs played the accompaniment, and she and Mrs. Selliger aided and abetted one another in triumphantly drowning little Mr. Selliger. Kit was rather sorry for him.

What a moldy evening it had been! And now she supposed she was in for another one, or something like it. As she pulled the limp folds of the Liberty frock over her head, she thought what rotten luck it all was. There was no fun in staying up late if you were let in for a beastly old musical evening. She picked up the string of yellow beads and fingered them thoughtfully. They were old ambers which had once belonged to Janey. Perhaps even musical evenings would have been different if Janey had lived.

As she kicked off her bedroom slippers and bent to find her sandals, Philip burst into the room. "I say, come on. Are you ready? The girls are going down."

She straightened herself quickly. "All right. Wait a jiffy. Will I do?"

"Do? Of course you'll do. What's all the fuss about, anyway? It's only old Papa Andreas."

He seized her hand and ran along the passage with her and down the stairs. The girls were just disappearing into the dining-room. "Supper's ready—Oh, be joyful!" he shouted, and leapt half a flight at a bound.

"Surely this is my Philip?" said a voice. Kit looked up sharply as she regained Philip's side. A stranger was standing in the hall with Charlie, a frail little man, slightly lame, with long white hair and sparkling eyes. "Philip, my dearest boy. Where have you been? Why all this brushing of the hair and washing of the hands?"

"Now then, Papa, you know what mothers are. And isn't it nice to see me clean and tidy for once? Come on, it's time for supper, and see here, this is Kit!"

Thus introduced with the supper, Kit very shyly shook hands. The old maestro looked down upon her benevolently. "Ah, child, I remember your pretty mother. I gave her a few lessons once, before your father came and ran away with her." He sighed and patted her gently on the shoulder.

"That's all right. Now let's get on with the eats," said Philip.

Kit wondered when the ceremonies were going to begin. She could not conceive of a musical evening without an imposing array of guests—all the people whom Laura simply *must* have because she owed them an invitation. Cousin Brenda did not seem to have invited anybody else. There was only the pupil, and he was not in the least formidable. He was a tall young fellow with a shock of red hair, a thin brown face, and strikingly beautiful hands. Papa called him Terry. Kit liked him, and so did Philip. He grinned at them over the supper table when they said that they wanted more tongue than chicken, and asked Cousin Brenda to give him the same.

After supper Charlie went to the Bechstein as usual. When she had done her share of the after-supper chores, Kit settled down to listen to him. He was playing a fugue, and as he gathered up the threads and brought it to a close,

Papa Andreas beamed approval. "You play well this evening, Charlie," said he.

"Oh, but Papa!"—Charlie swung round on the music stool eagerly—"Am I right to finish it off so? Mathers, the chap who teaches me, wants a 'rit.'"

The old maestro shrugged his shoulders. "He would. No, my boy, you should play it so. That is Busoni's rendering."

Charlie flung down the copy. "Come on, let's sing!" said he.

Kit's problem was solved. There was not going to be a musical evening. Nothing in the dreaded shape of a musical evening could possibly follow upon the Gramercie clarion call: "Let's sing!" She was so joyful in her surprise that she forgot the presence of the newcomers and sang away with the best of them. Cousin Charles joined in from time to time as usual, and Cousin Brenda beat out the rhythm over her mending basket with a darning needle, and the red-headed pupil, who had stretched himself out in the longest chair available, was irresistibly drawn in, too.

"Come, children," cried Papa Andreas. "You shall sing me the Angel Trio, and then Terry shall give you some lieder."

Philip shook his head. "I'd rather not, Papa," he confessed. "I've a bit of a throat, and my voice is beginning to break now, you know."

"Oh, Papa, it's a shame!" declared Milly. "He's only making a fuss. He can do it perfectly well if he wants to."

"That's all you know about it, young Em'ly!" protested Philip. "However, have it your own way since you're so clever—or—see here, let Kit take the seconds. She can sing it all right. I heard her only yesterday."

Self-consciousness was unheard of at Gramercie.

Without protest, Kit took her place between Milly and
Sheila. Her heart thumped furiously. "Lift thine eyes, O lift
thine eyes"—could she?—could she? She looked desperately
about the room. Cousin Charles had laid by his book, and
Cousin Brenda her needle. Philip had flung himself down
full-length on the hearth rug. He hadn't any doubt about
it, apparently.

Milly whispered in her ear: "Aren't you ready yet? Do you
want Charlie to give us the chord again?"

"Again," she whispered huskily—anything to gain time.

She thought of the times when she had tried to sing with
Pony and Helen, and how Pony had looked down her nose
at her. She thought of Elaine's song, and how bored the
others had been when she sang it. She remembered Martha—"Your mother sang so beautifully: it's a pity you can't
none of you sing like her"—and Laura—"Oh, Kit, do stop
making that awful noise! It's a pity you haven't got a nice
little voice like Daisy Trimble. Then perhaps we should be
asking you to sing." It was no use. She couldn't sing properly.
Everybody knew she couldn't, and everybody laughed at her.
She wanted to run right away, so that nobody could look at
her or laugh at her ever again. She wanted—who was that
looking at her? A pair of keen eyes, set deep in friendly
wrinkles, a firm mouth curved in the hint of a smile, one
slender hand half-raised, as if in beckoning—Kit's roving
imagination was captured and came to rest.

The Angel Trio rang out very sweetly in the long, mellow
room. Milly sang like a bird. She looked very lovely standing there, her fair head shining against the dark panelling.
Sheila sang carefully and well: she was no born musician.
Kit stood between them, looking straight in front of her. She
did not see the room or the friendly faces any more; only the

mountains of which she sang, whence help would come.

"Lift thine eyes, O lift thine eyes"—for the last time the three voices soared together. Peacefully they sank to rest, like birds gliding nestwards on quiet wings. Milly relaxed and crossed the floor to perch on the arm of her father's chair. Sheila made for the window-seat and her nibbled pencil stump. Kit did not move. She was still looking to the hills. Suddenly she came back with a little start, and stared about her, half-frightened. Cousin Brenda leaned forward and propped a cushion invitingly against her knees. Kit smiled gratefully and took refuge at her feet.

Papa Andreas rose slowly and limped towards the piano. "This must be a very good house," said he to Cousin Brenda with a little bow. "I always find something here to do me good. Come, Terry, have you anything for us?"

Terry reached for his Schubert. He was like the rest of them, thought Kit, he didn't waste time arguing. She wondered if he was a bass, like Mr. Campion, or a tenor, like poor little Mr. Selliger. He did not cough loudly, like Mr. Campion, but neither did he stand anxiously upon one leg, like Mr. Selliger. Perhaps he was something all to himself.

"He will begin with *An die Leier*," announced Papa Andreas. "And then—he will go on as he pleases. Eh, Terry? Are you ready, my boy?"

The maestro sat at the piano and the pupil stood in the crook, with one hand resting on the flap. They looked very much at home.

"This is a new sort of song," thought Kit. "This isn't like the Campions and the Selligers." She clasped her knees and leaned back hard against the cushion. Little phrases of the song sent ripples of enjoyment down her back. "I'm going to like this," she thought. "Oh, what a night!"

The next song was *Die Liebe hat gelogen*. Kit did not understand the words, but the music gripped her. The tragedy in it bit home until she could hardly bear the song. Was that music then? Something which could speak as terribly as that? Suddenly Kit realized what was happening. This was something bigger than Mr. Campion and Daisy Trimble and Mr. and Mrs. Selliger. "Just making a noise like they do, isn't singing at all, really," she thought excitedly. Singing was part of the "real me."

The song came to an end, but the singer still held the room. Papa Andreas turned the page with a smile. "Terry, my boy," said he, "some day you may be an artist!" and slipped quietly into the first bars of *Nacht und Traüme*. Kit closed her eyes. It was almost too lovely to be real. Musical evenings, and Miss Miggs, and Laura, seemed very far away.

The evening seemed to pass so quickly. There was *Die Forelle*, about a trout which you could almost see flicking its tail in the ripples of a rushing trout-stream, and *Gruppe aus dem Tartarus*, a terrible song which made Kit shiver. She did not know what it was all about, but that did not matter. She was sure there were writhing waters and thunder in it, and people in despair looking out over endless wastes for something which never came, and a great wheel going round and round for ever. Then there was *Wohin*, with a brook running through it, and *Der Musensohn*, which made her want to dance and sing, and *Erlkonig*, breathlessly exciting. After that came a quieter song, an old English folk-song. "I will give my love an apple," sang Terry, and then a house, and then a palace. Of course he would. He could give his love anything in the whole wide world. But he meant something more even than that, for "My heart is the palace wherein she may be, and she may unlock it without any key," sang

Terry, and Kit wondered when he would find her and what she would be like. He sang some more folk-songs, and then some sea shanties, and they all joined in the choruses, softly at first, in "Shenandoah," and then so riotously, in "What shall we do with a drunken sailor?" that Papa Andreas closed the lid of the piano and put his hands to his ears. But he was enjoying it, all the same. They knew that by the twinkle in his eyes.

"Children! Children!" said Cousin Brenda. "Don't you think that's a good one to end up with?"

"Not bedtime yet," they cried. "It isn't bedtime yet."

She laughed and ruffled her hair. "Only about two hours past," said she. "You've had a lovely evening. Don't spoil it."

Papa Andreas opened up the piano again and struck a quiet chord or two. "Come, Terry, you shall give them one more, and then we will say good-night. Which shall it be?"

"*An die Musik*," said Terry.

Kit started. That was the song of which Cousin Charles had spoken. *"Du holde Kunst, in wieviel grauen Stunden"*—yes, those were the words which Aunt Henrietta had whispered as she came upon sleep in that moonlit room at Belceaster House. *"Du holde Kunst, ich danke dir!"* That was the phrase which had stuck in her memory—*"ich danke dir"*—"I thank thee." It was only in music that Aunt Henrietta had ever really lived, and "I thank thee" was almost the very last thing that Kit had heard her say.

"Du holde Kunst, ich danke dir." As the song closed, there were tears in Cousin Brenda's eyes. Kit scrambled to her feet without a word and kissed her good-night. As she passed the piano, she held out her hand shyly, first to Terry, and then

to Papa Andreas. Papa Andreas held the little brown paw firmly in his long slender fingers. "Little Janey's daughter," said he, "will you promise me something?"

She nodded solemnly.

"Will you be like my Philip here, and sing, oh so *very* little, for the next few years?"

"Yes," she whispered, a little disappointed. Had she sung so very badly in the Angel Trio then? She made as if to slip away, but he would not let her go.

"And then, little Janey's daughter," he went on, smiling up into her face from the music stool, "will you sing for me again?"

11. *Heryot*

WHEN KIT RETURNED home to find Martha gone, she felt that nothing would ever be quite the same again. The kitchen did not seem like home any more. It was horrid to see Mrs. Perkins, the new "daily," with her long, mournful face and her perpetual sniff, sitting in Martha's chair. And it was worse still to feel that Martha was so far away. She had gone to see her brother in California, his wife had died recently, and there even seemed to be a possibility that Martha might settle there permanently. She had left a little note for Kit. It did not say very much, except just at the end: "Remember, my lamb, if ever you want me, I'll come." Kit wondered if Laura had read it.

Laura was very patient with Kit. She explained carefully that, with all the school and university fees to consider, as well as the Professor's researches, they must economize, and obviously, now that so many members of the family were away most of the time, Martha's expert help was not really necessary. "You must realize that I have had to sacrifice something, too," added Laura. "I have had to give up some of my committees."

"But I don't see the point," objected Kit. "We're not all away most of the time, by any means. Father's not, and I'm not, and anyhow Martha's one of us and everything will be horrid without her. Can't we—"

"But you are going to be away," interposed Laura tactfully. "I hadn't time to tell you in the middle of all the fuss at the station, but your father and I have decided to let you go to Heryot next term with Pony."

"Oh, Laura! Can I really?" exclaimed Kit. It seemed almost too good to be true. She had not liked the idea of returning to the High School without Pony, especially since Helen had told her that she would not be allowed to take her double remove. It would be much better to start again at a new school where nobody would fuss because she had been ill. And she had always known that some day she would go to the great Quaker school for girls at Heryot. The Haverards had been educated there, or at the boys' school at Marston, for generations. Most of them had, like her father, won their way there with scholarships. "Can I use my Junior Medal scholarship?" she asked.

"No, I'm afraid you can't," rejoined Laura. "It isn't transferable. And it's too late for you to sit for an Entrance Scholarship, even if Dr. Cray would allow it. So, you see, we shall have to sacrifice a good deal to send you there, and you really mustn't grumble if we've had to part with Martha."

"I'm sorry, Laura, but couldn't we have—"

"You can thank your lucky stars we've managed to get you in at such short notice," interrupted Laura briskly. "We only heard for certain two or three days ago. You weren't down to enter till the year after next, but Dr. Cray wrote and explained the circumstances, and they agreed to make a special place for you. You'll have to work hard, Kit, and show them you mean business."

"Of course I'll work. But it's all a bit of a rush, isn't it,

Laura? What about my things? I've grown out of all last year's undies."

"I ordered everything of that sort you'd be likely to need," said Laura, "just to be on the safe side. And I've sewn on all the name-tapes, too. That's a job you could very well have done for yourself, if only we'd had more time. Now I must measure you for your uniform and ask them if they can possibly rush everything through before the term begins."

"Is it a nice uniform?" asked Kit anxiously.

"It's a very practical one," said Laura, "though the girls seem to need more clothes than they did in my day. I'm sending you with the bare minimum: so long as your things are good and plain and sensible, they'll do."

When Kit looked into the chest of drawers where her outfit was stored, she decided that the things looked almost too good and plain and sensible. They would probably last for years, unless she could manage to grow out of them. She wished there had been time for her to help in choosing them, but perhaps it would not have made much difference. The vests were the kind Laura had always chosen for her, high in the neck with short sleeves. They were very warm and good, but Kit had been longing for sleeveless vests, like the ones Milly and Sheila wore. The pajamas were all in striped flannel, with long sleeves and plain collars. They looked very suitable for school wear, but Pony had floral ones, and Milly's and Sheila's were spotted and checked in all kinds of exciting colors. But at least every single garment had its name tape—J. K. HAVERARD in large red letters. She was thankful she had not had to sew them all on by herself. She did hope the uniform would come in time. She would hate to arrive looking different from all the other new girls.

The big box from the school outfitters was delivered in the

nick of time and it was a great relief when everything was assembled. The uniform looked very neat: grey gym-tunic and blue blouses, grey blazer, grey coat and skirt, grey Harris tweed overcoat, grey felt hat and grey beret. There were grey linen shorts for gym, and a blue silk tunic for Greek dancing. Blazer, hat-band and beret bore the school badge, a white fleur-de-lis on a blue ground.

"Why a fleur-de-lis?" asked Kit.

"It comes from the Mercy window in Heryot Cathedral," replied Laura. "A Heryot knight saved the life of a French prince when they were on pilgrimage, and the window was put up to commemorate it. There are white fleurs-de-lis all round the border. The school is supposed to teach international friendship, so it's rather suitable. But some people think it's because of Charles Lamb saying that Quakeresses were like lilies."

"Are all the girls Quakers?" asked Kit.

"Of course not," said Laura. "Heryot is a famous school and all kinds of girls go there. Mind you learn to get on with them all. You will, if you get rid of some of your odd ideas and learn to play hockey decently. Now what about sewing on these last few name-tapes? It's time you began to do something for yourself."

Laura was thankful to leave Kit anchored with the box of name-tapes, and get on with her work. She thought the child seemed thoroughly unsettled. She had noticed all sorts of little changes in her since she came back, and some of them she did not like. And she did wish Kit would tell her things: what was the use of looking after a child from babyhood if you were never to gain her confidence?

"You might at least look as if you were interested when I speak to you," Laura complained one day, when she was trying to explain the intricacies of hockey to Kit over the bed-making. "I don't know what's come over you. And do stop humming to yourself everlastingly as you go about. Anyone would think you were cracked."

"But I like to hear her singing round the house," protested the Professor mildly, as he came in search of a clean handkerchief. "I know nothing about these things, dear, but I have the impression that she can sing in tune."

"Anybody can do that, Uncle," declared Laura. "It's nothing to make a fuss about. Those people at Gramercie have been giving her a swelled head."

Tom was the only member of the family who was really interested in Gramercie. Richard had been away when Kit returned. Miles thought it all sounded too highbrow for words, his only consolation being that Kit would get some sense knocked into her at school. He was going back for his last year at Marston, and thought he might possibly manage to run over to Heryot occasionally, to see how the knocking process was going on. Meanwhile, he took every opportunity of strumming the latest American dance tunes on the piano when she was within hearing.

Tom was different. Tom asked questions. He had left Marston because he was too old to stay there any longer, but nobody knew what he was to do. His headmaster had observed politely on his report that he was "a keen naturalist and good with his hands." Laura shrugged her shoulders resignedly and suggested that he might try for a job on the land.

"All right!" said Tom one day. "I'll consider anything you like, but first of all I'm going to Gramercie."

"But that's ridiculous," protested Laura. "You can't afford to waste your time. Besides, they won't want you."

"Oh yes, they do!" rejoined Tom. "I wrote and asked Cousin Charles."

Tom had stayed on at Gramercie. A letter from him, to wish her luck, awaited Kit at Heryot. He had chummed up with Charlie and was having no end of a time. The Cathcarts had lent him a clarinet and he was learning to play it. He had been over to Belmouth to see Cousin Robert. Cousin Charles had let him spend a whole day working at Kitsons, and he was going to do it again. He liked it tremendously. Kit began to wonder. At the back of her mind, she was even a little jealous. It almost looked as if Tom had found his niche.

Kit and Pony travelled to Heryot with some older girls who were very kind to them and told them when they might eat their sandwiches. They were both very nervous, and for some reason or other their sandwiches tasted like sawdust. The other girls lent them some magazines, and later on they played a paper game. Kit had hoped that they would travel with Miles, who changed at Heryot Station for Marston, but Miles explained to Laura that it was quite out of the question, and even Laura understood.

"It simply isn't done," he said. "We never travel with the hags from Heryot."

"Not even with your sister?" asked Laura.

"Of course not!" declared Miles. "Least of all with sisters. I tell you, I won't do it, Laura. I'm going to be a prefect and I'm not going to turn up on the platform at Heryot with a couple of infant hags trailing after me. Let 'em learn to stand on their own feet and get it over."

Perhaps it was the best plan, after all. Kit thought she might as well take the plunge and be done with it.

When Kit arrived at the school, she found Tom's letter

awaiting her, and also one from Philip, wishing her luck. Pony had a pile of letters and post cards from her family and from her host of friends at the High School: one of the post cards was from Miss Miggs, and Pony tossed it over to Kit when she had read it. "Wishing my hard-working little pupil every success at her new school," read Kit, and handed it back to Pony with a shrug of her shoulders. Miss Miggs had not written to her, of course. Why should she? But music at Heryot was going to be different. Kit was quite sure of that.

Everything at Heryot was going to be different, of course. Nevertheless, the first day did not start very well. It was all so confusing, and she always seemed to be in the wrong place. She felt better when she was with Pony, so she sought her out whenever she had a minute to spare. Pony put up with her for a while, and then all of a sudden she made a best friend, and did not need Kit any more.

They were crossing the quadrangle with Pony's hockey stick and tennis racket. "I ought not to have brought the racket," said Pony. "They don't play tennis this term. Can't we stow it away somewhere?"

A thin, dark girl bumped into them and stopped to look at Pony. "Hullo, new girl, what's your name?" she asked.

"Ursula Cray," replied Pony.

"Is that what they call you?"

"No," interposed Kit. "We always call her Pony."

The dark girl ignored her. "I'm Bettina Endell. Everybody calls me Bendie. I like that racket you've got. Let me have a look at it. No, don't put your hand over the shield, silly. That's what I wanted to see. So you were Junior Champion at Chesterham, were you? That's not bad. Come along, and I'll show you where to hang it. Who's the brat you're trailing round with you?"

"Kit Haverard. She comes from Chesterham, too."

"Oh, does she? Well, she can't come with us. All the new brats are supposed to be queuing up for Matron."

"Oughtn't I to be there?"

"Oh, you're all right, Pony. You're with me. Come on!"

Kit was left standing alone in the middle of the quad. She had a panic-stricken feeling, as if everybody were looking at her. There were girls hanging out of the windows, girls running across the quad, girls calling to one another, teasing one another, using a new slang which she had not had time to learn yet. Then a quiet voice said: "What a bit of rotten luck!"

One of the older girls had stopped on her way across to the Senior Wing with an armful of books. She had a mop of fair curls and an elfin face. "Friend of yours?" she asked.

"Oh yes! She's Pony Cray. She's splendid. She was no end of a swell at the High."

"Was she? I'm glad you stick up for her, anyhow. Don't let Bendie put your nose out of joint. Like to carry some of these books for me?"

"I'd love to. But—don't I have to queue for Matron?"

"Oh, that's all rot! It'll do any time. You come and see my study. My name's Sylvia Felpham. They call me Flip."

Kit would have carried a ton of books for Sylvia. The first day at school wasn't going to be so bad, after all. But it looked as if music might not be the only thing which would be different at Heryot.

12. *Music at Heryot*

MUSIC AT HERYOT was quite simple when once you understood the rules of the game. People who were somebody learned with Tatty, and people who did not matter, learned with Old Fish. Kit was furious when she found that Laura had said that she was to go to Old Fish. Pony was learning with Tatty as a matter of course.

Mary Fishwick had been teaching the pianoforte at Heryot Friends' School in Laura's day and long before that. She was tall and grey-haired, with an aquiline nose, and she was one of the best disciplinarians in the school. Gillian Tattersall was a comparative newcomer, young and pretty, with smoky black hair drawn back into a little bun on the nape of her neck. She taught singing throughout the school, and had a host of pianoforte pupils as well. Her favorites would go to tea in her pretty room, where they would exclaim over the signed photographs on the walls: "All the best to Gill from Jack"—("He's a *wonderful* tenor, a second Caruso, but the critics won't notice him—so petty, don't you think?")—"For my darling little pupil, with oceans of love and best wishes from Loretta Cantilena." Old Fish had not so much as a post card in her room. It was severe and plainly furnished, with a copy of Beethoven's death-mask over the piano. Bendie said it gave her the creeps.

Bendie and Pony were as thick as thieves. It made things a little more complicated for Kit, but after all, she was used to that. Pony had always had a best friend at the High. Moreover, there was Flip in the background when things got too bad. The Senior Wing was forbidden ground, but somehow or other Flip seemed to know instinctively when Kit was in hot water.

"Kit Haverard!" somebody would call. "Sylvia Felpham wants you. You're to take her Beethoven up to her study. She says you know where to find it."

"What's the row about today?" Flip asked one afternoon, when Kit arrived with a very red face.

"Nothing. How did you know there was one?"

"Never mind. Tell me about nothing."

"Well, I was doing some extra practicing, and Bendie said I was putting on airs. She says I'm only one of Old Fish's pupils, and they're no good. She and Pony learn with Tatty."

"I know they do. Has it ever struck you that I learn with Miss Fishwick?"

"I've often wondered why."

"My uncle is a musician. He says Miss Fishwick is, too."

"But she's such an old frump."

"I know. And Tatty's so pretty. But just wait a bit and keep your eyes open. You'll see."

"But what about all those photographs in her room? She must know lots of famous people."

"So does Old Fish. Only they're not the kind who gush all over the landscape. You get to know her some day. I'm the only girl in the school who has ever bothered to do that, and this is my last year. I wish you'd have the sense to do it, Kit, instead of blahing about Tatty."

"I don't blah."

"Yes, you do! She's only to lift her little finger, and you start making goo-goo eyes, like the rest of the brats. You have a bit of sense and leave that kind of thing to your precious Pony and Bendie. Run along now, I'm busy."

"All right, Flip—only—I say—thanks awfully. I don't know why you're so decent to me."

"Nor do I. I think it's because you looked such a priceless idiot that first day in the quad. I was like that when I was a new girl. Now cut along, there's a good brat, and give me a bit of peace."

As she raced down the stairs, Kit nearly bumped into Miss Priestley, the Headmistress. She was touring the Senior Wing, with the inevitable Miss Binns in attendance. The girls all called Miss Amelia Binns "Fido," because she seemed to spend most of her life following Miss Priestley about.

"I think you are out of bounds, my dear," observed Miss Priestley mildly, blinking through her spectacles.

"I'm sorry, Miss Priestley," stammered Kit. "I've been to Sylvia Felpham's study. She wanted her Beethoven."

"I see. Sylvia is very kind to you, is she not?"

"Yes, Miss Priestley." Kit wondered how on earth Miss Priestley knew. She looked at her with dawning respect. The kind eyes which blinked behind the spectacles were unexpectedly shrewd.

"She is very musical, of course. I don't suppose you are. I remember Laura Haverard never got far with it. She was very good at hockey."

"I know. But Laura's only my cousin. She isn't my mother.

My mother died. Her name was Janey Kitson. She wasn't
a bit like Laura."

"No. I remember she wasn't."

"You knew her?"

"Yes, my dear. I come from Middlehampton, you know.
We're connected with the Spurriers. Janey Kitson often
stayed with them. You remind me of her, somehow. Now
run back to your playroom, and remember, next time Sylvia
sends for you, don't bounce down the staircase."

"Yes, Miss Priestley. Thank you, Miss Priestley." Kit
retreated in good order, and the Headmistress continued
on her way.

Miss Priestley had ruled over Heryot Friends' School for
years. There was a certain poetic justice about it, because the
establishment had been founded by her forbears, and the
original building, which now forms the entrance block, was
the Priestley family house. Jonathan and Rebecca Priestley
had founded the school in the eighteenth century, and long
after the control had been taken over by the Heryotshire
Quarterly Meeting of the Society of Friends, it was still
known as the Priestleys' Seminary. It is now the oldest
Quaker school in the world, and possibly the most famous.
It stands outside Heryot, high above the river, with a view of
the white-walled town and the Cathedral on the one hand,
and the rolling Heryotshire landscape on the other. Generation after generation passes through, and the influence of the
school extends far beyond the confines of the Society which
founded it. Its motto is taken from George Fox's writings:
"Walk cheerfully over the world," and many of its daughters
have borne it worthily to the far ends of the earth. Doctors,
nurses, teachers, missionaries and social workers had built up
a fine tradition long before Kit's day; she would sometimes

look a little wistfully at the carved memorial boards in the School Hall. There seemed to be precious little chance of her name ever appearing on one of them.

It was not until the end of her second term that Kit realized exactly what Flip had meant about Old Fish and Tatty. Bendie and Pony had been asked to tea in Tatty's room on Sunday afternoon, and told each to bring a friend. Pony brought Kit, as a matter of course, and Bendie brought a dumpling of a girl called Merle Peterson. Kit couldn't stand her. They had a good time together, all the same, though Kit felt a little out of it. She was the only one who was not a pupil of Tatty's.

Tatty wore a negligée of petunia-colored silk, and feather-trimmed mules to match. "You must make the tea, girls," she cried. "I'm tired out."

They persuaded her to lie down on the divan, and piled the cushions round her. Bendie, as the oldest, claimed the privilege of making the tea. Merle arranged the cakes, and Pony toasted the muffins. Kit was sent to fetch the bread and butter and milk from the buttery hatch.

They all clustered round the fire for tea, and took turns to wait upon Tatty. Kit handed her the chocolate biscuits.

"You knew Ursula before you came here, didn't you?" asked Tatty. She took the middle biscuit, the fat one wrapped up in gold paper.

"Oh, yes!" rejoined Kit. "We live quite near to each other."

"You went to school together, I suppose?"

"Yes, but we knew each other long before that. We've always known each other. We used to meet on Saturdays with another girl and play pretending—"

"Play *what*?" grinned Merle.

Pony shot a furious glance at Kit. "She means we used to rehearse plays sometimes," she explained hastily. "And we went for walks in the country, and that sort of thing, or practiced for the school sports."

"Pony won the Junior Sports Cup at the High!" interrupted Kit, anxious to make amends. She knew now that she ought not to have mentioned the pretending-games, but she could not think why. Only it would never do to fall out with Pony. She saw little enough of her as it was.

"Oh, shut up!" muttered Pony. "That wasn't anything to write home about. Don't be such a silly, Kit. What's happening after the match on Wednesday, Miss Tattersall?"

"We're to have a special concert. Didn't you know? Simon Trent is coming to sing for us. We're awfully lucky, aren't we? He came once before, and he was simply divine."

"Are you going to accompany him?" asked Pony.

"Oh no, of course not. Don't be such a little silly. Miss Fishwick always gets the accompanying. She's been here much longer than I have."

"But why should that make any difference?" protested Bendie. "You play far better than she does. You know you do."

"And you'd look lovely on the platform," sighed Merle. "You could wear that sweet chiffon frock. Oh, can't you do it just this once?"

Miss Tattersall shrugged her pretty shoulders. "It's no use, dears," she said. "We mustn't upset Miss Fishwick."

"I think it's the limit," stormed Pony. "She's just being a dog in the manger, keeping you out of things."

"The old cat," sneered Bendie.

"That's just what she looks like at the piano," laughed Merle. "An old cat. She must have been wearing that black lace dress of hers for years."

"Oh no, she hasn't!" tittered Miss Tattersall. "She had another one when I first came."

"Had she? What was it like?" they all asked eagerly.

"It was—*another* black lace dress."

They all laughed uproariously. Just then somebody knocked at the door. Kit ran to open it. Miss Binns stood anxiously on the threshold.

"Do you want me, Miss Binns? Shall I come?" asked Tatty, sitting up on the divan.

"Oh, please don't trouble, dear!" Miss Binns implored her apologetically. She called everybody "dear"; Bendie could imitate her to perfection. "It's only about Wednesday."

"What's the matter?" asked Tatty, blushing unexpectedly.

("Old Fish can't play. Hurrah!" whispered Bendie.)

"It's so awkward with Miss Priestley away. I don't know what to do. Poor Miss Fishwick has gone to bed with influenza and the doctor says she can't possibly be well in time. I know you don't like to play in public, dear, but if you could—just this once? It's so late to ask him to bring his own accompanist—and then—the expense—with Miss Priestley away—she doesn't return until late tomorrow night. Do you think you could manage it, dear?"

Tatty hesitated. All eyes were on her face. She cleared her throat. "Of course, Miss Binns!" she said brightly. "He'll send the music, I suppose?"

"Oh, yes, dear. It should be here by Tuesday morning, I think. Thank you so much, dear. Don't let me disturb you any more, girls. What a happy party!"

Kit closed the door behind her. Pony and Bendie somersaulted round the room. "*What* a happy party, dear!" they shrieked. "Good for Fido! Congrats, Tatty darling!"

They all danced round her and crowned her with a cake frill.

"May I turn over for you?" asked Bendie. "Oh, *say* I can turn over for you. Flip always does it for Miss Fishwick, and it's time somebody else had a turn."

"It ought to be somebody in the senior school," hesitated Tatty.

"That's only one of Miss Fishwick's notions," laughed Bendie. "What does it matter who does it, anyhow? It's nothing, to turn over. Most of the seniors would rather listen, I should think. And I do so want to do it. Please."

Tatty gave in. "Of course you shall," she laughed, and began to hand round the chocolates. Kit nearly missed hers when her turn came. She was thinking about something else. "I know you don't like to play in public, dear!" Whatever could Fido have meant?

By the time Wednesday came, all Tatty's pupils were wild with excitement. Simon Trent arrived during the afternoon, in time for a rehearsal. Nearly everybody was on the field, watching the match, but Kit had to come away early, to fit in a practicing half-hour. Tatty brought him down to the Big Music Room to practice, and Kit stood in the corridor to see them go by.

"I need somebody to turn over at the rehearsal, Kit," said Tatty. "You'd better come."

"I'm really supposed to be practicing, Miss Tattersall," said Kit.

"Oh, that doesn't matter!" declared Tatty impatiently.

"We oughtn't to take her away from her work, ought we?" suggested Simon Trent with a smile.

"I'd like to come," volunteered Kit. "I'll fit in the practicing

another time. Only wouldn't you rather I fetched Bendie, Miss Tattersall?"

"Gracious, no!" said Tatty. "She wouldn't thank you for taking her away from the match."

"I think we ought to be introduced," said Simon Trent kindly, as they were sorting out the music. "My name is Simon Trent. What's yours?"

"Kit Haverard."

"Haverard?" He stopped and looked at her for a moment. "Where have I heard that name recently? Oh, I know!—a nice young fellow at the Cathcarts. Tom Haverard, he was called. Plays the clarinet. He was living with the Kitsons at Gramercie. Any relation of yours?"

"Oh yes, he's my brother. Our mother was a Kitson. And Sir Hugh Cathcart is Cousin Brenda's father. How lovely to think that you know them all. Do you know Papa Andreas, too?"

"Of course I do! I'm a pupil of his. Where did you meet him?"

"At Gramercie. The last evening I was there." This was the loveliest thing that had happened since she came to school. She was just going to tell him all about it, when Tatty interrupted them. She was looking rather annoyed.

"Have I got them all in the right order?" she asked abruptly.

"Oh yes! I'm sorry. Only Kit and I seem to be old friends. We'll start with the Scarlatti. I'm not going to sing out."

"Shall I miss out the introduction?" suggested Tatty.

"Goodness no! It's part of the song."

"Very well. But don't be alarmed if I make mistakes. When you come in, I'll follow you. And of course it will be all right tonight."

Simon Trent bit his lip. When he came in, he sang *sotto voce*. There was hardly any tone, but every note was perfectly pitched and formed. He went through two groups in this way.

"I wish he'd sing out," whispered Tatty. "I can't follow him at all. He makes me nervous."

Kit wondered at the back of her mind whether an accompanist could be much use if she "followed" you. Surely, if she accompanied, she was supposed to be going *with* you. But it was not really anything to do with her; her job was to turn over, and she concentrated on that. It was a pity Bendie was missing the rehearsal. Turning over was not as easy as it looked.

"Didn't you see the note on the copy?" asked Simon Trent, as Tatty started another introduction. "I like that a tone higher."

"Oh, I'm so sorry—I didn't realize—I'm afraid I don't care much for transposing."

Tatty floundered on for a bar or two, until he interrupted her again. "I think we'll cut it out, Miss Tattersall. I'll sing this one instead, if you don't mind. It should balance the group pretty well."

Just as they were beginning the third group, Miss Tattersall remembered that she had promised to ring somebody up at four o'clock. "Excuse me," said she. "I'll not be a minute."

Simon Trent went on singing to himself.

"How do you make that into a big tone?" asked Kit.

"Breath!" he replied. "Listen, and I'll show you."

He sang a note with the smallest volume imaginable, then steadily filled it out and rounded it with breath, until the room echoed with sound.

"That's what lies at the back of all singing," he explained. "Just put your hands here and feel."

Kit felt the swell of ribs and diaphragm as he inhaled, and then the slow, steady release of breath into music.

"See?" he asked, smiling down at her. "If ever you want to sing, you must first learn to breathe. Don't you forget it. Now, tell me, what on earth's happened to Miss Fishwick?"

"She's got influenza. She's still in bed."

"Well, I only wish they had let me know, that's all."

"Is she so very good?"

"Good? Heavens, yes! Don't you know it?"

"I ought to. I learn from her. But all the girls are crazy about Tatty."

"They are, are they? Well, you remember this. The sooner you stop bothering about what all the rest of 'em think, the better. Miss Fishwick's a genius. I don't know anything about her teaching, of course, but she's a born accompanist, and they don't grow on every bush, as you'll find out some day, when you're older. Now then, let's get on with the job."

Tatty came back apologetically and they finished the rehearsal somehow. "I shall be all right tonight. Don't you worry," laughed Tatty.

Simon Trent bowed. "I should advise you to ask Kit to turn over," he suggested. "She knows the program now."

"Oh, but I promised Bettina!" Tatty expostulated. "She's one of my best pupils. She'll do it beautifully."

"Very well!" said he. "I'll take a stroll round the grounds now, before I go to my room."

In the evening, Kit was very glad that she had not been asked to turn over. It would have been terrible to sit there, helplessly watching Tatty make mistakes. There was a difficult passage in one of the modern accompaniments where she was only playing the first note in each bar. Simon Trent went on as if nothing was the matter. He even went on when Bendie dropped the music. Of course, she would have known all about the turn-back if she had rehearsed it: as it was, she fumbled forwards and backwards, and the copy slipped to the floor. Tatty looked furious and Bendie went as red as fire. But Simon Trent never so much as turned his head.

As he went down the corridor afterwards with Miss Priestley, Kit heard him say: "Thank you, Miss Priestley. I'm glad you've enjoyed it. Only next time I come, if Miss Fishwick is indisposed, would you be so very kind as to let me know."

"Of course I will!" said Miss Priestley. "I should have done so this time if I had not been away. She is the only real accompanist we have."

A bevy of Miss Tattersall's favorites flocked with her to her room. Merle had bought some flowers for a bouquet. "You looked so lovely, Miss Tattersall," she simpered. "Your dress was perfectly sweet."

"Was it?" asked Tatty eagerly. "I'm so glad. Of course, it was terrible having to play at such short notice. It simply wasn't fair of them to ask me. Especially when the man wouldn't even rehearse properly."

"Wouldn't he?" they chorused. "What a shame! Never mind, you were wonderful, darling."

"He didn't give me a chance. He wouldn't even stop when Bendie dropped the music. I could have slapped you, you little wretch. But it was his fault for not marking his music properly. Never mind! Let's all have a chocolate before you go to bed."

Next morning, as Kit was finishing her compulsory early morning run, she met Simon Trent coming up from the San.

Male visitors generally stayed there if there was no epidemic.
"Good morning, Mr. Trent," she called to him.

"Good morning, Kit," he replied. "I'm just going to snatch
some breakfast with Miss Priestley before I catch my train.
What are you doing? Running round the garden? That's
good for your breathing!"

"Is it? I say, when are you coming again? I want to hear
you sing some more."

"Do you? Well, I can't say when it will be. But I can tell
you one thing."

"What's that?"

"I rather think you'll be doing the turning over."

13. *St. Merlyon's Chapel*

HELEN JOINED PONY and Kit in the summer term. Her work at the High School had suffered since they had left, and Dr. and Mrs. Cray had persuaded Mrs. Edgington to give up the idea of Penart Close and send her to Heryot Friends' School, where an unexpected vacancy had occurred. She had no difficulty in settling in. But then, Helen could make herself at home anywhere, Kit thought.

If it had not been for Helen, Kit might have felt a little out of things, for Pony was in great demand for tennis and cricket, and Flip was busy with examinations. However, almost as soon as Helen arrived, she developed a craze for archaeology. She made friends with a blonde sixteen-year-old called Peggy Withers: Peggy specialized in brass rubbings, and was only too glad to have two companions in her walks. Helen decided to specialize in stained glass, and spent hours pondering over the windows in the old Heryot churches whilst Peggy scrabbled on the tombstones. Kit was quite content to do nothing in particular. When the other girls asked her what she had been doing, she said that she had been "getting a general impression." It was a very useful phrase.

Later in the term, they decided to start on the Cathedral.

They would need the whole of the winter to work on it, but it seemed the best idea to make a start while the light was good. Helen and Peggy were very systematic about it and worked steadily to plan. Kit had no plans at all until she found that, if they went on half-holidays, they could hear part of the evensong and yet be back in time for tea.

There was a little chapel in the south aisle of the chancel, dedicated to St. Merlyon. It reminded Kit of Gramercie. It was cut off from the aisle, first by the back of a big tomb, and then by a little grille with a padlocked gate. If no vergers were about, and if, like Kit, you were very thin, you could just squeeze round between the edge of the tomb and the first bar of the grille. Then nobody could disturb you, and you could listen to the singing to your heart's content, without being asked what you were doing, or if you wanted to be shown round. You didn't even have to be interested in the progress of Peggy's rubbings, or Helen's latest discoveries in the glass. And if things had been pretty rotten, and Bendie and Merle rather more than usually objectionable, well, you could get away from that, too.

The tomb was an interesting one, when you got to the other side of it. An Elizabethan gentleman and his lady lay side by side, with folded hands; the hands were beautifully modeled. Their children knelt below them in stiff little rows. The inscription ran: "Here lye ye bodies of Nicholas Chauntesinger and of Alice his wife, good citizens of this city and faithful servants of this church, beloved alike for their benevolence and their virtue, to whom their seven sons and five daughters have raised this monument in filial piety and in certain hope of the resurrection. A.D. 1601." Kit liked the name "Chauntesinger." She often wished that Pony still played pretending-games. She would have loved to play at being a Chauntesinger.

She was sitting in the little chapel one summer's afternoon, trying to straighten things out in her mind. She had
quarreled with Bendie that morning, and Pony had taken
Bendie's side. She had gone across to the Music Wing to
do some extra practicing before breakfast, and finding the
Big Music Room empty, had gleefully taken possession. It
had the best pianoforte in the Wing, very few of the others
were much good. Bendie had appeared almost immediately
afterwards, and had tried to turn her out. She had declared
that Kit had no business to be there at all, only people in
the senior school were supposed to practice there, and
some of Tatty's best pupils. Tatty had told Bendie she could
go any time she liked. Pony had joined in, and had made
things worse by telling Kit that it didn't matter, because
she couldn't play for toffee in any case. Eventually Kit had
appealed to Old Fish, who had "squashed" them all with
chilly impartiality by quoting an old rule which said that
the Big Music Room piano was to be kept locked, the key
was to be available to the senior girls only on application to
the senior music mistress. Miss Priestley agreed that it was
a pity the rule had been allowed to lapse. All Tatty's pupils
were furious with Kit. Pony said she hoped she was satisfied
with the results of her blabbing. Kit tried to tell Helen all
about it, but she could not understand why on earth they
were making such a fuss. Flip was too busy revising to be
much concerned.

Kit sat in a corner of St. Merlyon's Chapel with her chin
resting on her hand. She was beginning to feel better about
things. Suddenly she heard the sound of a key in the padlock
of the grille. There was nothing she could do about it. There
wasn't so much as a niche where she could hide. She simply

sat on and hoped for the best.

The head verger stood back respectfully as he opened the gate. An elderly man in a black cloak came stumping in.

"What's this? What's this?" he exclaimed. "Grierson, I thought you never let anybody in here alone."

"I don't sir. I don't know how the young lady has got in, sir."

"Please, he didn't let me in, truly he didn't. I got in round the corner of the monument. I can just do it. It's easy if you're skinny. I'm sorry if it's your tomb—your chapel, I mean."

"My tomb, indeed! D'you hear her, Grierson? My tomb! Impudent little hussy!"—(his voice went up into a squeak with sheer indignation)—"I suppose that's the kind of manners we must expect from that confounded Quaker school."

"My manners aren't anything to do with the school," flared Kit. "If they're bad, that's my own look-out. I said I was sorry, didn't I?"

"Come, come, miss! you mustn't answer back," expostulated the verger. "This is Sir Geoffrey Chauntesinger."

"I'm sorry," repeated Kit firmly. "But I can't help getting annoyed when people criticize my school, can I?"

"No, you can't!" said Sir Geoffrey suddenly. "What do you come here for, anyhow?"

Kit hesitated. "Oh, I just sit and think," she mumbled.

"Don't believe it! Nobody thinks, these days. Turn out your pockets."

Bewildered, Kit fished out three pocket handkerchiefs in various stages of dirtiness, a halfpenny, a pencil stump, a stick of sealing wax, a bit of string, half a dozen cigarette cards and a black-currant lozenge.

"I thought she might be coming here to chew toffee,"

explained Sir Geoffrey to the astonished verger. "Next time, let her in through the gate."

"Do you mean I can come here again?" asked Kit.

"Yes. Come whenever you like. It's a long time since I met a young person who wanted to think. Now you can come back to tea with me."

"It's very kind of you to ask me, but I can't," declared Kit boldly.

"And why not, hey?"

"I must go back with Helen and Peggy. We shall be late enough as it is." She could see them signaling desperately in the crossing.

"She knows her own mind," announced Sir Geoffrey. "That's what comes of thinking. But I know my own mind, too. So you'll take this card to your headmistress, my dear, and tell her that I detest her school and all the Quakers that ever quaked into the bargain, and will she please send you to my house for tea next Sunday. D'you understand, hey?"

His voice ran up into a squeak again. Kit noticed how his eyes twinkled under his bushy eyebrows. "Very well!" she grinned. "Thank you very much. I hope my manners will have improved by then."

"Hm!" said he, as he shook hands with her. "I think I prefer you as you are."

Miss Priestley smiled over the card, and still more over the message. "You are very privileged, Kit," said she. "I have never been to tea with Sir Geoffrey Chauntesinger. He has a lovely old house."

"Who is he, Miss Priestley?" asked Kit.

"He's a famous architect. He was knighted for his work on the Cathedral, when the center tower was in danger, twenty years ago. They say nobody else could have saved it.

His family has been in Heryot for centuries. He knows more about the Cathedral than anybody else. It's a pity you're not one of the archaeologists, Kit."

"But I go archaeologizing every week," protested Kit. "I go with Peggy Withers and Helen Edgington. Peggy's done some lovely brass rubbings."

"I know," said Miss Priestley quietly. "But that is not what you go for, is it?"

Kit stared at her and said nothing. Miss Priestley always knew so very much more about you than you thought she did.

Her visit to the Chauntesingers was a great success. They lived in a big gabled house behind the Cathedral. There was a courtyard in front of it, and a velvet lawn. Two statues dreamed over the flower beds, one of a goat-legged boy with panpipes, and one of a girl with a lyre. The boy reminded Kit of somebody, but she could not tell who it was. Inside, everything was unusually beautiful, even for Heryot.

"Visitors often come here by mistake and ask to be shown round," explained Cathy Chauntesinger. "They annoy Father terribly, but when he's out of the way, we show them round for fun. Sometimes they try to tip us, and if Father hears about it, he goes up in smoke."

Cathy and Rose Chauntesinger were very kind to Kit. Cathy ran the house and everybody in it, Rose nursed her mother, who was delicate. Lady Chauntesinger presided over the tea-table from her invalid chair. Kit fell in love with her at first sight.

"So you like that confounded school of yours, do you, hey?" growled Sir Geoffrey as he stirred his tea. Four lumps in a Dresden china cup. Kit wondered if he could see land.

"Of course I do!" she replied. "It would be funny if I didn't.

The Haverards have been going there for generations."

"You have, have you? Hang it, surely you're not Quakers?"

"Yes, we are."

"Good Lord, and I thought you looked as if you had some sense. I said I'd never let a Quaker set foot in my house—until—well, I said I wouldn't."

"I'll go now if you like," suggested Kit politely, and took a large mouthful of cake. It would be a pity if she had to leave it behind.

"Of course you mustn't, dear," said Lady Chauntesinger mildly. "Geoffrey, please don't."

"It's all right, I don't mind," interposed Kit hurriedly. "I expect you do think we're rather funny. I used to think so myself when I was little."

"You'll think so again one of these days," snorted Sir Geoffrey.

"No, I shan't," declared Kit roundly.

"Then why do you sit mooning in St. Merlyon's Chapel? Hey?"

"I don't moon, any more than you do. I come for a bit of peace. We don't get much at school. And I like the music. But I can't think why you let all those trippers chatter and giggle and fidget about. It's so much lovelier when it's quiet."

"So you're attacking me in my own camp, are you, hey?" Sir Geoffrey smiled at his daughters. "She's a bonny little fighter, isn't she?" he remarked.

"She knows how to stick up for herself, anyhow," said Cathy. "Tell us some more about the school, Kit. We often look at it as we drive past."

After tea, they showed her round the house. When it was

time for her to go, Lady Chauntesinger beckoned to her to come close. "I hope you weren't hurt, my dear, by what Geoffrey said about the Quakers?" said she, a little anxiously.

"No," replied Kit. "If that's what he really thinks, well, there's no sense in being hurt about it, is there?"

"No sense at all, Kit. Because it is Sir Geoffrey who has been hurt, not you. He felt it very much when our boy threw up his course, to study music, and still more when he began to go to the Friends' Meetings, in spite of his father's disapproval. It was all because of a visit he paid with his singing master to some friends of his who were Quakers. And now he has given up architecture entirely, and it is a great grief to his father."

Sir Geoffrey stumped in and Lady Chauntesinger kissed her good-bye. "You'll come again, Kit, won't you? And didn't you say you had a brother at Marston? Wouldn't you like him to come, too?"

"I'd love it!" said Kit. "We don't often go out together. He could cycle over easily. And if we came one Sunday, there wouldn't be a match. He's Captain of the Cricket Eleven, you know, and a Prefect as well. He won't be there next term. He's going to London to study medicine."

"Hope he sticks to it, that's all," growled Sir Geoffrey. "Now you can go back to that school of yours and tell Mrs. Pussy, or whatever her name is, that you're to come again."

"Shall I bring her next time?" suggested Kit, grinning.

"Goodness, no! She'll be trying to turn me into a confounded Quaker. Now, get along with you, and I'll look out for you sometimes at St. Merlyon's Chapel."

Miles and Kit were asked to go one Sunday late in the term. Miles was a little doubtful about accepting, but eventually Kit persuaded him. She had been invited to Marston for the Old Scholars' match, and they had only time to snatch a few words together afterwards. "You must come, Smilo," she had insisted. "We've hardly seen each other today. You can't let this be the last binge."

"I don't know why not," protested Miles. "After all, I shall probably see a sight too much of you in the hols."

"No, you won't, silly! You're always going off for camps and treks and goodness knows what. And I shall be at Manningleigh and Gramercie part of the time."

"So you will. When does Tom get off, I wonder? He's coming on the senior trek with us. The Head asked him. I believe Laura's furious because he'll not be at home much of the hols."

"I don't think Laura likes the idea of his going into Kitsons. But I think it will be splendid. Philip doesn't want to—he told me so ages ago—and Tom and Charlie get on so well together."

"I think old Tom's landed on his feet," said Miles. "And have you heard that Richard's been offered a lectureship at Prince's?"

"That's great! "declared Kit. She knew it was. But they were all growing up, and she was left behind. Even Miles would be grown up when he left Marston. "*Do* come to the Chauntesingers, Smilo."

"All right." After all, thought Miles, he had better look in and see the folk that the brat had been palling up with.

It was a very jolly tea party. Cathy and Rose seemed to like Miles very much. It was just beginning to dawn upon Kit that he was good-looking. She had even caught Merle Peterson taking his photograph.

"Our boy has come home for a week or so," explained

Lady Chauntesinger. "I'm afraid he and his father are late for tea. They have been to evensong."

They heard the door open, and the sound of voices in the hall. "What did you say, boy? Can't hear a word you say. Why can't they teach you to speak up, with all this singing? Hey?" Sir Geoffrey's voice rose to an impatient squeak.

The reply sounded very good-humored. And there was something familiar about the tone of the voice.

"Come up to your mother and the girls," said Sir Geoffrey. "And I believe that dratted little Quaker is here with her brother. You ought to meet her. She's a quake 'em and no mistake."

"Come along, Father! We can hear every word you're saying," laughed Rose.

The door opened, and Sir Geoffrey stumped in. Behind him came a tall young fellow with a mop of red hair and a friendly grin. He was not unlike the faun in the garden.

"Why, it's Terry!" exclaimed Kit.

"What—what the—how the dickens do you two come to know one another?" squeaked Sir Geoffrey.

"Quite simple, Father! We met at Gramercie. That was the first time I went there. This is the girl who sang in the Angel Trio. I told you about her. I thought she was one of the Kitsons."

"I am, really," explained Kit. "I'm called Kitson Haverard."

"What's all this about Angel Trios?" cried Miles. "Kit isn't an angel, by any means, and she can't sing. She makes a ghastly row."

"She never told me she could sing," growled Sir Geoffrey. "Whoever heard of a Quaker who could sing, anyhow?"

"You'd better sing for them, Kit!" suggested Terry, as if it was the most natural thing in the world.

Kit blushed furiously. She wished she could sink through the floor. If only they would all get on with their tea.

"Come on!" urged Terry.

"No use asking a Quaker to sing," muttered Sir Geoffrey. "They don't know what it means."

But she did know what it meant. She knew far better than he did. It was finding the "real me." It was the kind of thing that Doctor Cray was getting at when he told her about people speaking in Meeting. You couldn't explain it, unless perhaps you explained it when you sang. The little folk-song came into her mind; she pitched it instinctively.

> *As I was a-walking*
> *One morning in the spring,*
> *I met a pretty damsel,*
> *So sweetly she did sing.*
> *And as we were a-walking,*
> *Unto me this did she say:*
> *There is no life like the ploughboy's*
> *All in the month of May.*
>
> *The lark in the morn*
> *She will rise up from her nest.*
> *And mount up in the air*
> *With the dew all on her breast.*
> *And like the pretty ploughboy*
> *She will whistle and will sing,*
> *And at night she will return*
> *To her own nest, back again.*

"Dash it, the child can sing," exclaimed Sir Geoffrey.

"Why on earth didn't you tell me, brat?" asked Miles.

"Sing us some more," urged Cathy and Rose.

Kit shook her head. Lady Chauntesinger understood. "Let me cut you another slice of cake, dear," she suggested. "And we must have some fresh tea. Sit down, Geoffrey dear. It will be ready in a minute."

Sir Geoffrey sat down heavily and helped himself to the teacakes. "Who would have thought it?" he mumbled, over the first buttery mouthful. "That dratted little Quaker."

14. *"She will rise up from her Nest"*

THE NEXT YEAR, Kit spent the greater part of the summer at Belceaster House with Aunt Maria and Aunt Priscilla. Laura had gone to join the Professor in Crete. Secretly, Kit had longed to go, too. She saw so little of her father, even in the holidays. Laura thought it was a ridiculous idea. She considered that the Professor was spending a good deal more on his researches than he could properly afford. That was his own affair, of course, but she was not going to sanction any extra unnecessary expense if she could help it. Fortunately, his vague suggestions that perhaps Kit might care to join them during the summer holidays were made only to Laura; it was easy to put a stop to them by pointing out how bored the child would be. And as Kit's home letters were always read aloud by Laura over the breakfast table, it was equally easy to miss out the passages which contained the veiled hints. Laura wanted to have the Professor to herself for one thing, and for another, she did not want to be bothered with Kit.

"You oughtn't to let that cousin of yours have her own way so much," insisted Philip one day, as he and Milly and Kit were idling in the "wilderness" at the bottom of the Belceaster House garden. "She bosses the whole lot of you,

146

so far as I can see."

"She's always been very good to us," acknowledged Kit slowly. "She's looked after us ever since Mother died."

"That's all very well, but it's no reason why you should all eat out of her hand," said Philip. "I believe Tom shivers in his shoes every time he gets a letter from her. I can't think how he managed to pluck up enough courage to defy her and come into Kitsons."

"That's different," said Kit. "That's the kind of thing you just have to decide for yourself."

"Is it?" scoffed Milly. "Well, you don't seem to be in a hurry to decide anything, do you? But then, of course, you're always a worm where Laura is concerned."

"I'm not," declared Kit stoutly. "I can't help it if she doesn't like me as much as the others, can I?"

Philip looked at her for a moment. He was growing up fast now, whereas she still seemed to be a kid. "It isn't that, exactly, is it?" he suggested. "Isn't it something to do with Aunt Janey?"

Kit flushed. "Perhaps it is. Laura was very fond of her, I think. Richard says she was. I often think she's disappointed because I'm not like her."

"You're a bit of a fathead, aren't you?" observed Philip. "Can't you see that the trouble is that you're growing more and more like her?"

Kit shook her head. Philip might be very clever, but what did he know about Janey? Or Laura either, for that matter? "Laura has always been very good to us," she repeated firmly. "I don't know what we should have done without her."

"All right, have it your own way," said Milly, airily dismissing the subject. "What's going on at Heryot, Kit? Do you like it as much as ever?"

"Of course I do," replied Kit. "There are ups and downs, of course, but that's all the same wherever you are. And I'm jolly glad I went when I did. I should have hated going back to Chesterham High School without Pony."

"Is she your best friend?" asked Milly.

"Not exactly," said Kit. "I've never had a best friend. But—well, she's just Pony. And there's Helen—the one that's coming to stay here—we three have always been together. We've lots of other friends, of course. Heryot isn't cliquy, thank goodness."

"It sounds a pretty decent sort of place," admitted Milly. "If I have to change schools for Higher Certificate, I shouldn't mind going there myself."

"I think a dose of Heryot would do you good, Milly," teased Philip. "You want knocking off your perch a bit!"

"Oh, shut up!" flared Milly. "It would take more than boarding-school to knock some people off their perches! Come on, Kit, let's go and help to get tea ready."

Philip and Milly came over often whilst Kit was at Belceaster House, and sometimes they brought Sheila with them. She still wrote endless stories. On the day when Helen was expected Philip came early in the morning by himself, and suggested a long walk across the downs. Kit thought they would have plenty of time for it before she went to meet Helen at the station; she would not be likely to catch an earlier train than the one which arrived at three o'clock. They hurriedly collected lunch packets in the kitchen, and set out by the path which led up the hillside behind Easingholme Farm. It was a hot day. By the time they were half-way up the slope, even Philip was glad to pause for breath.

They stood for a moment, looking down at Manningleigh. They could still see Belceaster House and the other old houses round the Place. Beyond, half-hidden by trees, was the spire of the old church. As they rested there, they could hear the church clock striking twelve. It was a quarter-past ten by Philip's watch.

"Has that clock ever been right?" laughed Philip.

"Not so far as I can remember!" said Kit. "I should think there was something wrong with it, if it were. Nothing ever changes in Manningleigh, Philip. That's one of the things I like about it."

"But it's going to change," frowned Philip. "Everything has to change. In another ten years, you'll hardly know the place. Look at the buses that have started to run right through from London to Belmouth."

"I hate them!" declared Kit. "I want everything to be as it was when Mother knew it. Nothing had been changed when I first came here, except for a few motor cars. Now they've built a garage in the High Street, with a row of petrol pumps. I hate it. Don't you, Phil?"

"Why should I?" he replied. "People have to have petrol, don't they? And nobody wants Manningleigh to be a museum. It's time you stopped looking for something in the past, Kit. Try thinking about the future for a change."

Kit shook her head. "I don't want to. You don't understand!" she said. She hated it when Philip talked like that.

They walked a long way along the ridge of the downs, until they could see the towers of Belceaster Cathedral in the distance, rising above the red roofs of the town.

"It looks as if you could pitch a stone over there," remarked Philip. "But you couldn't, not by a long chalk."

"In the old days you would have seen the spires of St. Merlyon's Abbey too, wouldn't you?" said Kit. "It must have been very lovely then."

"There you go again!" said Philip. "It's lovely now, isn't it? Times have to move or we'd all be as dead as mutton. Personally, I like Gramercie better as it is."

"There's nowhere else like it, is there? Do you remember that first time I came to stay with you? Such a lot of things seemed to begin then."

"They did. We shall always remember that, I suppose. Terry Chauntesinger says he will, too. Do you see him often when you go to the Chauntesingers, Kit? Odd fish, isn't he?"

"He isn't. He's a very good sort. Miles likes him no end."

"Miles does, does he? How very nice for Miles!"

"It's funny, because they're not a bit alike. And Miles says he doesn't care for any music except jazz. He's always teasing Terry about it. But Terry doesn't mind a bit; he just grins and says Miles is a silly idiot and that's why he likes him."

"So you're a silly idiot too, are you?"

"Why?"

"Well, he likes you, doesn't he?"

"I don't know about that. I see much more of his father than I do of him. Sir Geoffrey calls me 'that dratted little Quaker.' But he's all right if you stand up to him."

"Most folk are, Kit. That's why you'd get on a sight better with Laura if you stood up to her."

"I don't know what you mean, Phil!"

"I know you don't. But you will, one of these days. And I only hope you find it out in time."

They lay up there for a while, sprawling full length on the turf and lazily dipping into their lunch packets. The sunshine was beginning to make them feel sleepy. Philip dozed off for a few minutes; Kit was humming drowsily to herself, with a grass stalk between her teeth. He would always be her special friend among the cousins, she thought. But soon he would have to stop laying down the law to her: she was growing up. At last he yawned and turned over. She jumped up and began to collect the rubbish. "We ought to be getting back," she said. "I've got to meet Helen's train. Won't it be a sell if she comes by the earlier one after all?"

"Helen's one of the special friends you told us about, isn't she?" asked Philip.

"She and Pony are. Aunt Maria asked them both to come, but Pony's with her people, of course."

"And Helen?"

"Well, they're different, you see. Her mother and sisters like to go and swank somewhere. This time they're coming to Belmouth, so they're parking Helen here. They're only too glad to be rid of her, I suppose."

"Why?"

"Well, she's clever and plain, like her father, instead of pretty and daft, like them. You won't need to tell *her* to stick up for herself, Phil. She has to do it all the time, or she'd never get anywhere."

They hurried back as fast as they could. When they reached the bottom of the lane, they found Helen waiting for them.

"Miss Kitson told me you had gone this way," she said. "Don't bother, Kit. I didn't think you would be there to meet me. We came earlier than we expected. It was so hot in the London shops that the others thought they would hurry on to Belmouth."

Helen was wearing a green linen frock and sandals. The fresh breeze from the downs had blown some color into her thin, clever face. "This is my cousin, Philip Kitson," explained Kit. "Philip, this is Helen."

"I thought you said your friend was plain," said Philip afterwards, when he and Kit were alone together for a few minutes.

"Her people all think she is," said Kit.

"Well, they must be a queer lot! Because she isn't, not a bit of it. Is she, Kit?"

"She's a good sort, is Helen," said Kit non-committally. How anybody with Milly for a sister could consider Helen as anything but plain, was a mystery to her. All the same, she was glad Philip appreciated Helen. So few people did.

When Terry Chauntesinger came over to spend the week with the Cathcarts, their circle seemed to be complete. They met at Gramercie or Belceaster House nearly every day and went on long walks together. Sometimes Tom and Charlie joined them, but usually they were too busy at Kitsons. The summer holiday season was always a rush for them. Milly and Sheila came, of course, and sometimes they would even drag Cousin Brenda away from her typewriter and persuade her to come, too.

It seemed very quiet at Belceaster House when Helen had gone. Aunt Maria and Aunt Priscilla missed her as much as Kit did.

"She seemed almost like one of the family," declared Aunt Priscilla.

"So she did," said Aunt Maria quietly. "Perhaps that is because she is not happy at home."

"She isn't, but how did you guess, Aunt Maria?" asked Kit.

"When you have lived as long as I have, it is easy to guess," said Aunt Maria. "And easier still to know. Thou has the picture of Sophia and Henrietta and Susan still, hasn't thou, Kit? Would thou say that Henrietta looked a happy child?"

"N—no!" confessed Kit. "But Helen won't grow up like Aunt Henrietta, will she?"

"Not if she wins her freedom, dear. And that is easier to do now than it was in our young days."

"You talk as if you want everybody to break away from their families, Aunt Maria. But that wouldn't be right, would it?"

"It is the only right thing to do. We must all break away before we can come back. Like the little song thou sings about the house: 'And at night she will return to her own nest, back again.' But she must rise up from the nest first."

"But you didn't break away, Aunt Maria, did you?"

"Of course she did not, dear child," declared Aunt Priscilla. "It would have been very uncomfortable for us all if she had. Dear Maria has always been so dependable. Ever since dear Sophia died. And I think it is a great mistake for young people to dash about so much. It would be much better for them all to stay quietly at home. Now I must go and see if I can find another ounce of the pink wool. I meant to ask Philip to buy me some more in Belceaster, but he has not been to see us since dear Helen went away."

After she had gone, Kit repeated her question abruptly. "*Did* you break away, Aunt Maria?" she asked.

"Yes, Kit, in my mind. I have always kept my freedom within. And if you do that, there is something within you which nothing can touch."

Kit thought of Doctor Cray. They all seemed to come back to the "real me" idea in the end. "That's what the Early Friends believed, isn't it?" she asked.

"It is what we all believe, but we cannot have it unless we

seek it and follow it. And that is what some of us are afraid to do. Remember that, dear child."

Kit drew nearer to her. "Used you to talk to Mother like this?" she asked.

"Often," said Aunt Maria. "And when the time came, she 'rose up from her nest.'"

"But she didn't come back," said Kit bitterly.

"Ah, but she will!" said Aunt Maria gently, and her wise old eyes rested on Kit's face.

15. *A Man's Life*

SIMON TRENT did not come to Heryot again until Kit's third summer term. They did not often have concerts in the summer, but this was a special occasion. There had been devastating floods and epidemics in West China, and the school was heading the town effort to raise a fund to relieve the suffering. Two Old Heryot Girls were working with the medical mission on the spot, which added to the local interest.

Miss Priestley had suggested giving a public concert in the School Hall. It was capable of holding a very large audience and the acoustics were excellent. The girls were to be packed into the back seats. Simon Trent had promised to come, and he was to bring Rudolf Brenner, the famous Hungarian violinist. Brenner had recently acquired a Stradivarius for four thousand pounds, and the papers were full of it. "Rudolf Brenner to visit Heryot with his £4000 Strad"—"Famous Violinist brings priceless Strad to Heryot Friends' School."

"What a lot of rot!" snorted Pony when she saw it. "As if any old fiddle could be worth so much."

Pony was nearly sixteen now, and she and Helen were in the Fifth. To their mutual astonishment, Pony was at the bottom of it this term, and Helen at the top. But Pony was Captain of the Form.

"I don't know so much about 'rot,'" said Kit. "If I were a violinist, I should want to have the best fiddle I could get."

"Oh, you *would*!" rejoined Pony. She hated it when Kit "put on airs" about music. As if she knew anything about it, anyhow! After all, she was still only one of Old Fish's pupils. Everybody knew that Old Fish had all the duds. And Tatty did not think much of her singing, whatever those people at Gramercie might say. It was so awkward and unbalanced, as if she could not control the tone. Tatty always chose Merle Peterson for the solos; she had a sweet little voice. Sometimes she even chose Pony. She liked Kit to sing seconds, because she could at least be depended upon always to sing in tune; Pony suspected that yet another reason was because it kept Kit in her place.

"If I were a down-and-out," observed Helen, "I should feel a bit sore about that four thousand pounds. I quite agree that it's right for Brenner to have the thing, but I don't think the newspapers ought to make such a song about it."

"Perhaps somebody'll pinch it!" suggested Pony hopefully.

"No such luck!" grinned Helen, who did not really want to go to the concert at all. "You couldn't get rid of the thing if you did pinch it. Nobody's going to buy a stolen Strad."

When you came to think of it, nobody would. Helen always seemed to have the last word. They rolled over on their rugs and fished hopefully for bulls' eyes. Pony had brought some down from her tuck-box, but they were nearly all gone. It was a hot Sunday afternoon, and they were all lying on the edge of Near Field, writing their home letters.

"I shall have to write to Tom as well," sighed Kit. "What a nuisance it is when the family is scattered all over the place. It's much easier when everybody's at home and one letter does the lot. But he wrote to me twice last week. By the way, he says Milly and Sheila will be coming here next term."

"Bless us, Milly's as old as I am, isn't she?" said Pony.

"She's coming to do Higher Certificate," explained Kit. "She gets across the Senior English Mistress at Belceaster Grammar, so she wants to come here for it. And Sheila doesn't want to stay on there without her, so she's coming, too. I think Milly's a bit hipped because Phil's going away. He goes up to Cambridge next term. He's awfully brainy."

"I thought he was too cocky for words when he and Milly stayed with you," said Pony. "I liked Milly though."

"Depends what you mean by cocky!" said Helen. "Some boys are like that when they're clever. Girls don't usually get the chance: they're too good at being sat on. But I like Philip very much, all the same. Does he still play the fiddle, Kit?"

"Yes, he does. Shall I pinch the Stradivarius for him?" laughed Kit. "Or perhaps Mr. Brenner will give it to me, as the concert happens to be on my birthday!"

The day before the concert, Kit went up to Miss Fishwick's room for her music lesson, and found her studying a pile of music. Kit had not quite stepped into Sylvia Felpham's place with Miss Fishwick. She always vaguely resented the fact that Old Fish was not pretty and charming, like Tatty. And she was not an inspiring teacher, by any means. She worked her pupils hard, and gave them a good grounding, but somehow Kit suspected that they had not much to show for it all in the end. Tatty's pupils got precious little grounding, but they enjoyed life.

"Is that the music for tomorrow, Miss Fishwick?" asked Kit.

"Yes. It seems I shall have to play for both of them. I thought perhaps Miss Priestley would engage a professional accompanist. It's rather a tall order, Kit."

"But Simon Trent wouldn't have anybody but you, I know. He thinks you're a genius."

"Does he?" Miss Fishwick laughed a little bitterly. "It's obvious you don't."

Kit hesitated. This was not the Old Fish she knew. But she suspected that Flip was right; very few people ever really knew Old Fish. There was something frigid about her which scared you. She had never forgotten one miserable morning in her first term, when she had passed up her porridge plate at breakfast and asked politely: "Please may I have a little more fish, Miss Porridge?" Miss Fishwick had not spoken for the rest of the meal. And it was no use trying to explain.

"I think you play beautifully, Miss Fishwick," she said candidly. "Especially when you accompany. I think Simon Trent meant that you're a genius as an accompanist. And I can't judge that, can I?"

"That's very straight," said Miss Fishwick. "I'm glad you don't slop over me like Miss Tattersall's pupils do over her. Would you care to turn over for me tomorrow?"

"I'd love to!" acknowledged Kit. "If you're sure it oughtn't to be one of the older girls."

"Very well. You must wear your white frock, of course, and see to it that your hair is tidy. And remember, your responsibility is to do your job well and be inconspicuous. None of my pupils in the Sixth can tackle it decently; they're all either too cocksure or too fussy. I haven't had a good turner-over since Sylvia Felpham left."

"She was awfully good, wasn't she? I'll do my very best to be like her. Shall we be able to rehearse?"

"That's a sensible question. Most of them think it isn't necessary. Yes, we'll be rehearsing tomorrow afternoon. Sorry to spoil your half-holiday."

"I don't mind. May I look at the music now?"

"Would you like to run through it with me?"

"Of course I would!"

"Then I'll give you extra time next week for a lesson. Give me the first group, please."

As she reached across the piano, Kit's hands brushed over Miss Fishwick's. "How cold your hands are!" she exclaimed.

"Of course they are!" said Old Fish. "Don't you know what it is to be nervous?"

"But you're not nervous? Not the day before?"

"Better the day before than the day itself, child. No accompanist can afford to have nerves on the day. Now then, we'll begin."

When they had finished, Kit arranged the music neatly in the various groups. "That was even better than a lesson, Miss Fishwick," she said. "I feel I've learnt a tremendous lot about the program. And I never thought accompanying was so important."

"That's the trouble with you young folk. You don't think. And precious few accompanists do, either."

"Why couldn't you just be an accompanist, Miss Fishwick?" asked Kit. "You *are* one, aren't you?"

"You can't be anything that's worth while unless you're prepared to take risks," said Miss Fishwick, biting her lip. "I wasn't, I suppose."

At the Saturday afternoon rehearsal, they ran straight through the program. Simon Trent smiled when he saw Kit by the piano. "I said that was what you would be doing, Kit. Do you remember?" he asked. Old Fish seemed to understand his *sotto voce* better than Tatty had done. She played the accompaniments exactly as if he had been singing full voice. Kit tried to be as deft and noiseless as possible when she turned the pages, or changed the music on the piano. Old Fish nodded approvingly. She did not seem to be at all nervous now.

Rudolf Brenner was older than Simon Trent, a little, square man with a bush of dark hair. Kit loved to watch him with his Strad. It seemed to be part of him, just as Simon Trent's voice was part of him. When he had run through possible encores, he turned to her. "You like my playing, hein?"

"I love it!" she replied. "And I've never heard a fiddle like yours. I wish—I wish I could hold it in my hands."

"You shall. But only for a minute—so! No longer! There, you have held my life! You could not hold Simon's life, could you?"

"Not unless she throttled me!" laughed Simon Trent, and they went off to the San together, to rest and change.

"I think I'll go and lie down, too, before I dress," said Old Fish. "Don't forget to give your hair a good brush, child. It always looks so untidy."

The concert was a thrilling experience. Kit sat like a mouse in the green-room and watched the performers. Rudolf Brenner walked restlessly up and down. Simon Trent kept on disappearing into the cloakroom to gargle. Old Fish smiled as she caught Kit's eye. "They have their nerves on the day of the concert, but before the performance!" she said.

"We accompanists can't afford to wait so long. Never mind, they'll be all right when they get started."

"But surely they've performed at all kinds of grand concerts," said Kit. "Why on earth should they be nervous here?"

"It's my private opinion that they would be every bit as nervous if it were a Sunday school treat!" Old Fish replied. "They're all like that. If they're not, they're no good."

When the time came, Kit opened the door for Rudolf Brenner, and slipped in quietly behind Miss Fishwick. She prepared the music during the first roar of applause. She felt almost as tense as the performers. She knew that the Chauntesingers were sitting in one of the front rows, but she dared not look at them. Nothing mattered except the job in hand.

It was a magnificent program. The *Heryotshire Post* reporter scribbled enough notes to fill a couple of columns: he even noticed that "the accompaniments were played in a masterly fashion by Miss Mary Fishwick." Privately, he thought that the kid who did the turning over had rather a striking face, but he supposed that would not interest his readers. He asked one of the girls what her name was, and wondered if he would ever hear it again. He happened to have asked Pony, and as befitted the solemnity of the occasion, she gave it in full: Jane Kitson Haverard.

After the concert, Kit could not go to sleep. She began to wonder if she would be awake all night. Everything had been so exciting. And even though she had had to slip away at the end, when the Mayor and the Dean and Sir Geoffrey Chauntesinger all came to be introduced to the performers, they had insisted on saying "Good-bye and thank you!" to her, before they let her go. Old Fish would have slipped away, too, if Sir Geoffrey had not stopped her. "Must shake hands with you, Miss Fishwick," said he. "You seem to have done most of the work, hey?"

"We're very lucky to have such a brilliant accompanist on our staff," said Miss Priestley. "You may run away now, Kit, but I want you to go straight to the kitchens and ask Miss Maddocks for some milk and biscuits. I do not think you had any supper."

Miss Priestley always seemed to know everything, thought Kit. And you would never guess it, by the way she blinked amiably behind her spectacles.

For a while she read in bed surreptitiously, by the light of her flashlamp. It was against the rules, but that could not be helped. All the other girls in the dormitory had gone to sleep. It grew later and later. She heard the school clock strike eleven and then twelve. It was a beautiful moonlight night.

Her eyes ached with reading, and the flashlamp was giving out. At length she pushed the book under her pillow and put on her dressing-gown. She might as well sit up and look out of the window for a bit. She crept past the other beds and climbed on to the high windowsill. Her dormitory was at the corner of the block; she could see right down to the river, beyond the school walls. Underneath the window stretched the girls' gardens, and beyond them were the San Garth and the San. There were no lights in the San windows. Rudolf Brenner and Simon Trent would be asleep by now. She sat there for a long time.

Suddenly she saw a dark figure emerge from the shadows of the little wood beyond the San. She did not know that the gardener ever went on his rounds so late. She had often tried to keep awake to see him go round at eleven. Generally he had his dog with him. This time he was alone. He crept round the San, feeling at the windows, and then disappeared round the other side. It seemed rather funny, Kit thought. And then she suddenly remembered what Helen had said. "If I were a down-and-out, I should feel a bit sore about that four-thousand-pound Strad!"

She glanced round the bedroom. Ought she to wake anybody up? If she did, they would all wake up, and there would be no end of a row if it turned out that she was making a fuss about nothing. She caught sight of Bendie lying asleep, her dark hair straggling over her face. Bendie would be sure to say something beastly. It would be horrid after such a red-letter day.

She slipped out of the room. The window in the corridor outside opened on to the fire escape. It would not take a minute to climb down and find out for herself. She could not go back to bed and do nothing about it, just in case—! After all, it was the man's life. He had told her so.

There was a big drop at the bottom of the fire escape; she was terrified of it. She reached across to one of the drain pipes and scrambled down it, grazing her hands and knees. Then she pattered across the school gardens and into the San Garth. She wished she had thought to put on her bedroom slippers.

After that, everything happened in a flash. She saw the man jump from one of the San windows with something under his arm. "Help! Stop thief!" she screamed, and then remembered in the back of her mind that all the people in *Oliver Twist* had shouted "Stop thief!" when they were chasing Oliver. He hadn't had a dog's chance.

She did not wait for anybody else. She ran as fast as her legs would carry her, into the little wood where the man had gone. She would never have caught him up if he had not lost his way. As it was, she cornered him by the wall. She could hear confused shouting and footsteps in the distance.

He caught her by the arm. "Show me the way out!" he panted. He looked very young. He could not have shaved for nearly a week.

"I will if you give me the Strad," she whispered hurriedly.

"Strewth! Wot d'yer think I pinched it for?"

"I know, but you couldn't sell it. Somebody would be sure to recognize it. You can't get rid of things like that. Don't be an idiot. Give it to me!"

"This way! They went this way!" shouted Rudolf Brenner in the distance.

"Give it to me, I say! It's that man's life! You can't take it away!"

"Can't I? Wot abaht mine?"

"Yours'll look pretty silly if you land up in quad! Come on, I'll show you how to get out."

There was a tree farther down the wood; you could scramble up it and drop down the other side of the wall. Girls who were "gated" used it if they wanted to break bounds. It was a pretty near squeeze. As he climbed over, he looked down at her.

"You won't split?" he said.

"Of course not. I've got the Strad!"

"It's a man's life!" he said, and disappeared. Kit knew it was something she would never forget.

Simon Trent found her shivering in the undergrowth, clutching the Strad. "I've got it!" she said, and her teeth began to chatter. He picked her up and carried her back to the San. She would not let go of the fiddle until she saw

Rudolf Brenner. "It's all right!" she said weakly. "Can I go back to bed now?"

"Not in those damp pajamas!" laughed Sister. "Come along, childie, you're spending the night with us."

A quarter of an hour later she was sitting by the fire, wrapped up in blankets, with a steaming mug of hot milk. Simon Trent and Rudolf Brenner had warm drinks, too, and so had Sister and Nurse, and various other people who seemed to have turned up in the meantime. They all laughed and joked, and drank her health, and Kit felt more and more as if she were in a dream, until Sister whipped out her thermometer and packed her off to bed.

She spent most of the next week in the San, and often she would waken screaming in the middle of a nightmare, in which a young, unshaven face would glare down at her from the sky. She could see it so clearly that she could have drawn it when she woke. But the funny thing was, that when the police questioned her about the burglar, she could not tell them anything at all about him. It had been so dark under the trees, apparently, and everything had happened so quickly. It was no wonder that she could not remember. And after all, it was a man's life.

16. *Facing the Music*

B Y THE TIME Kit came back into school from the San, most of the fuss had died down.

"I believe Sister kept you out longer on purpose!" declared Merle. "There were reporters who wanted to take your photograph and everything. Miss Priestley said we weren't to give them so much as a snapshot."

"They got hold of one, all the same," grinned Bendie. "I know who gave it to them!" She winked at Merle.

"I wish they hadn't!" declared Kit. "I hate all this fuss."

She did hate it, really. And she liked the way Pony and Helen went on just as if nothing had happened. Still, it was rather nice to have Bendie and Merle following her about. And Tatty had changed completely.

"I want you to come and have tea with me by yourself one day, Kit," she said shortly afterwards. "We never seem to have a chance to get to know one another, do we?"

They had a chat over the teacups in her room, and Tatty showed Kit all her photographs, and talked about her student days. "Of course, I had to specialize on the piano," she explained. "It's so much more useful for teaching. And I hadn't any choice about the teaching. My uncles wouldn't hear of anything else."

166

"What a shame, Miss Tattersall! Why did you bother about them?"

"They were my guardians, you see. They were always so hard on me. Sometimes they were really unkind. Perhaps they didn't mean to be, but they just didn't understand."

Kit vaguely remembered two stout, middle-aged gentlemen who occasionally came to visit Tatty, and who always attended speech days. They had not seemed unkind at all. One of them had tipped Pony half a crown. It all showed that one could never tell.

"What would you have done if you'd had your choice, Miss Tattersall?" she asked.

"We—ll, I *could* have been a pianist, you know. But it wouldn't have been any use. My poor nerves would have let me down. I'm so sensitive, dear. Even the pupils' concerts at college used to upset me. Otherwise, everybody said I should have won the gold medal. No, I could never have played in public. But singing—perhaps—if it hadn't been for my health—well, we never know, do we? I gave up singing at college. The teachers there had no soul. I think Uncle Ben must have been a teeny bit sorry for the way he'd always treated me. When I went to Madame Cantilena, he let me send him all the bills. Oh, Kit, she was perfectly divine!"

"That's her photograph, isn't it?"

"Yes. Wasn't it darling of her to write on it like that? You have read it, haven't you? She used to be simply sweet to me. Of course, she knew all about my difficulties. She used to say I'd have made a perfectly lovely Mimi in *La Bohème.*"

"Why didn't you have a try at it, Miss Tattersall? Surely your uncles wouldn't really have minded?"

"Oh, but you don't know how troublesome they were! And then, of course, my voice is so delicate. But Madame

Cantilena used to say I was *perfect* in old French chanson-
ettes. If only I'd had the chance, I might have been another
Yvette Guilbert."

"What a shame! Still, you do like being here, don't
you?"

"I love it, of course. You girls are all perfectly sweet to
me. So are some of the staff. I never feel that Miss Priestley understands me; but then, you couldn't expect a strict
Quaker like she is to appreciate anybody with an artistic
temperament, could you?"

"Yes, you could. What about Miss Fishwick?"

"Well, she's always been rather a stumbling block, my
dear. Of course, you won't repeat any of this, will you? But
she has been here so long, and—"

Something in Kit's face made Tatty stop in mid-flight.
The girl looked as if she might shut up like an oyster. That
was not what Tatty wanted at all. No, she would have to
leave her to Old Fish. But surely she could cash in on the
excitement in some other way. Especially if Old Fish had
not the sense to do anything about it.

"It seems such a pity that all my singing should go for
nothing," she complained.

"But you teach all the singing in the school!" protested
Kit.

"That's different. You can't call class singing *"singing"* can
you, dear? Now, if only I could give some singing lessons!"

"I thought you couldn't train girls' voices until they were
nearly grown up," said Kit. "Most people wait until they
leave school, don't they?"

"Jenny Lind didn't. She began when she was nine."

"Oh—Tatty—wasn't she lucky?"

"I suppose—I suppose your people wouldn't like you to

have singing lessons?"

"Goodness, no! I don't suppose Laura will ever want me to have them. She thinks it's a waste of time unless you're really good."

"But you *are* good, Kit! It's only just that you don't know how to use your voice properly, and I could soon teach you that. Can't we do something about it? Supposing you sang at a concert here so well that everybody raved about you? Wouldn't Laura change her mind?"

"She might. But I don't think she would. And I don't suppose I would either—start everybody raving, I mean!"

"You just try it and see. I haven't much time, but I'm sure I could spare a few half-hours to coach you. Then perhaps, at the end of next term, or the term after, we could surprise them all."

"Do you really mean it? Would you give me lessons?"

"Of course I would!" Tatty could see the whole plot unfolding into the future. It would make a lovely story for the newspapers—("Schoolgirl Rescues Stradivarius: Beautiful Young Teacher Discovers Phenomenal Voice: Teaches for the Love of her Art," etc., etc.) Then there would be the stage of acknowledgements: "I owe all that I have done to the gifted teacher who first encouraged me." She would be able to set up a studio on the strength of it, and wouldn't Uncle Ben and Uncle Joe be mad? Only Madame Tattersall did not sound right somehow; she would have to invent another name. "Gillianova" wouldn't be bad.

Kit did not tell anybody about the lessons. It was all going to be a surprise. For a few miserable weeks in the autumn term, she thought nothing was going to come of it after all, for Milly created a sensation when she arrived as a new girl, and Tatty was so excited when she discovered that she was a granddaughter of Sir Hugh Cathcart's, that she forgot all about Kit. Everybody knew that Sir Hugh was the greatest composer of his generation. He had just been given an O.M. The annoying thing was that Simon Trent appeared to have told him all about Old Fish. He had not even mentioned Tatty.

Everybody liked Milly. She was so lovely that nobody could help it. She went about with Pony and Bendie and Merle, and Kit sometimes felt a bit left out. Pony had failed badly in School Certificate, so badly that she was to take another year over it. Her father had insisted that the only thing for her to do was to start all over again, and Miss Priestley had agreed with him. She had been the only unsuccessful candidate from the school.

Pony had come rushing round to Kit when the results came in the summer holidays. "They're all so good to me at home," she wailed. "I can't bear it! It's all my own silly fault!"

"No, it isn't, Pony. It's just a bit of rotten luck. You can't be good at everything."

"What about Helen?"

"She isn't good at games like you. And she's nothing like so popular."

"I don't care. I know it's all my fault. You don't know how I've been slacking. I thought I could pass easily. Oh, Kit, can't you see that I've been getting my head turned?"

That was the kind of conversation to which you never referred afterwards. You could never "let out" like this except to your very oldest and closest friends. Suddenly Kit knew that Bendie and Merle and the rest of them did not really matter at all.

"Don't let it get on top of you, Pony," she had said. "You

must rub it out and begin again. If you let it get on top of you, you'll never be rid of it. I don't mean to let anything get me down, ever, if I can help it. I remember Phil always used to say: 'Nothing matters, so long as you've got guts!' Pretty beastly way of putting it, but it's true."

Pony had cheered up then, and they had gone for a tramp round the park. Builders were hard at work in the fields where they had once played together. "Do you remember *that*?" asked Kit, pointing to the wall and the gnarled hawthorn tree. "Somehow or other, nothing ever seemed to be the same afterwards."

"It wasn't!" said Pony. "Funny, isn't it? And all we were bothered about was whether we should be back in time for dinner."

Kit liked having Pony in the same Form, but she knew it was a bit of a come-down for Pony. She was Captain, of course, but the girls who used to follow her last year were now in the Lower Sixth. And everybody was making a fuss of Milly. She was every bit as good at games as Pony, and the prettiest girl in the school, into the bargain. Nobody noticed Sheila much, except Kit. She was still writing stories.

Tatty was disappointed when she found that Milly would not be having pianoforte lessons. But apparently she would have been learning with Old Fish in any case, so it did not make much difference. She took violin lessons with the visiting mistress: Kit thought she was beginning to play almost as well as Philip, but she did not put so much feeling into her music. Soon Tatty found that she had a voice. She made her sing solos in class until Merle was nearly green with envy. "My dear, I've made a discovery!" she declared one day to Kit, who had come to her room, hoping for a lesson. "That child has a natural coloratura! With those looks and such a voice—What a Rosina! What a Gilda!"

Some people had all the luck, thought Kit. She didn't think that she herself had any looks at all. Certainly her brothers did not seem to think so. She had grown considerably of late, and her hands and feet seemed to be all over the place. Her dark hair was thick and glossy, but she had not any color to speak of. Milly was all pink and white, like a rose.

One way and another, Tatty's concert was put off, but at last there came an opportunity, towards the end of the spring term. Some of the girls wanted to organize an entertainment in aid of the Fresh Air Fund, and they asked Tatty to help them. It was to be an ordinary school concert, but parents and friends could be asked.

Kit worked hard for weeks beforehand. Tatty had decided that she was to sing Mozart's *Voi che sapete* from *The Marriage of Figaro*.

"Don't you think it's rather too difficult for me?" asked Kit doubtfully.

"Not a bit of it. It's easy. See what a simple little tune it is! There's nothing in it. And if you just get up and sing little folk-songs, nobody will know that you can do anything."

"I suppose not. But what about the words? Do you think anybody could lend me an Italian dictionary, so that I could have a shot at translating them?"

"Nonsense! The words don't matter. They never do in that kind of song."

Kit had no difficulty in learning the tune. Reading music was easy enough. But she thought it was a little high for her. Tatty laughed at her. "Smile on the high notes and they'll come easily!" she said. It certainly was easier if you smiled. Only Kit wondered what the effect would be if the song happened to be a tragic one. She still found some of the high passages difficult, and Tatty showed her how to alter the vowel sounds. That was a great help, too. Only it sounded a little as if she were singing in a broad Heryotshire dialect. When they came to the last line, Tatty wrote an alteration.

"Oh, but I oughtn't to alter Mozart, ought I?" exclaimed Kit.

"Why not? Madame Cantilena always took a B flat there."

"I suppose it must be all right if she did it. But I can't sing as high as that, anyhow."

"Of course you can, silly! Take it on 'ah' and don't bother about the words. And remember to smile. All singers like to get a high note at the end of the song."

Kit was growing more and more doubtful. But if she said anything, Tatty would be cross. And she could not ask Miss Fishwick; Miss Fishwick was not interested in the concert at all. It was Tatty's affair entirely. She would have liked to have talked it over with the Chauntesingers, but they had all gone away for a change after influenza. They hoped to be back in time for the concert.

Kit had never thought that there would be any trouble about walking on to the platform. Tatty had never suggested such a possibility. But when she walked in through the green-room door, she hardly knew which way to go. She stumbled over something on the stage, and somebody laughed. It sounded like Bendie. A titter went through the audience. She blushed and looked helplessly at Tatty. She had not the faintest idea what to do with her hands.

Tatty played the introduction rather too quickly. Kit sensed that she was nervous, which did not make things any easier. She nearly came in at the wrong place. She looked down at the front row and saw the Chauntesingers. Terry was with them. Oh, why had he come home, this week-end of all times? And why had they brought him to the concert? He looked up at her encouragingly, and suddenly she knew that she must not funk it. She must go through with it, now that she had started.

Her voice sounded rather thin in the big hall. If only the song had not been quite so high, it would have been much better. She smiled on all the high notes, as Tatty had taught her, but she could not help feeling that it made her look rather silly. Most of the vowels had been turned into "ahs" and "ows." They were easier to sing that way, of course. But she was terrified of the B flat at the end. Why, why had Tatty made her put it in? She dared not miss it out. Tatty would be furious if she did. Besides, she was going to play a chord with a flourish while Kit held it. Her voice seemed weaker and weaker. Tatty was playing so fast that she had scarcely time to take any breaths at all, let alone deep ones. If only she could have sung something simple! She was nearing the end now. Here it came! She squeaked despairingly, with a grin like a Cheshire cat, but she had not hit it properly. She scrambled to the end as best she could.

She did not wait for Tatty or anybody else. She raced along the corridor and out into the garden. She knew she was supposed to join the audience at the back of the hall, but she did not care. Nothing mattered any more. Milly and Bendie and Merle and a host of other girls were clapping like mad, to hide their giggles. Let them laugh! She would run away from school that very night.

Somebody caught her roughly by the arm and she struggled to get away. Her other arm was caught in the same masterful grip and it was no use trying any more. He swung her round to face him. "Come back at once!" said Terry. "You can't run away."

"Terry," she gasped.

"I pretended I had to come away early. I knew what you would be up to. But you've got to face the music. Pull yourself together!"

She bit her lip. "But—please—Terry—"

"You meant to run away and have a good howl. But you can't. Not until afterwards. You don't want people to be *sorry* for you, do you?"

"No, I don't! You're a beast, Terry! It's only that I've made such a mess of things—"

"No, you haven't. It's that fool of a woman who's been teaching you. She has been teaching you, hasn't she?"

"Yes."

"Well, promise you'll never let her teach you again!"

"All right. I promise. She won't want to, anyhow. Can I go now, Terry?"

"No. You've got to promise me something else. Next time you come south, you're to see Papa Andreas. Promise?"

"I couldn't, Terry. I'll never sing again. I'll—"

"You're not going to let them down you, are you? Dash it, Kit, I thought you'd a bit more in you than that!"

(Nothing matters so long as—) "All right, Terry, I promise."

"Now you're going into the audience. Nobody will know that you've been away if you slip in at the back."

But when they reached the door into the school, Miss Binns was waiting for them. "Sneak!" thought Kit. "*Sneak!* And I shall never be able to explain. Nor will Terry. She'll never understand."

"Miss Priestley sent me to look for you, dear!" said Miss Binns cheerfully. "She doesn't want you to stay outside in the cold too long."

Miss Priestley again—how did she know?

"I—er—I thought I had better come out and fetch her back, Miss Binns," stammered Terry, awkwardly.

"That was very kind of you," said Miss Binns composedly. "Thank you so much. I think Kit had better go back into the hall now; she will just be in time to hear her cousin Milly sing 'The Lass with the Delicate Air.' You ought not to miss it, dear. Slip in quietly at the back and nobody will notice you. Perhaps, Mr. Chauntesinger, you would rather wait for the others in the car outside?"

"Yes, I would, thanks, Miss Binns." Terry watched Kit run noiselessly away down the corridor. "You're very kind, Miss Binns," he said suddenly. "You seem to understand."

"My dear boy," she said gently, "I have been here a very long time."

Milly sang "The Lass with the Delicate Air" like a bird. Everybody was so busy congratulating her afterwards, that Kit's fiasco was almost overlooked. She rushed up to the dormitory without waiting for the others, so that she could be reading in bed by the time they came up. She lay awake for a long time after "lights out."

Next day, she overheard them all laughing in the cloak-room. Tatty was going round inspecting for afternoon tidiness.

"Oh, Miss Tattersall darling, you should have *seen* her!" squealed Merle. "She looked so f—f—funny!" She collapsed into helpless giggles.

"I heard her and that was enough!" laughed Tatty. "Wasn't it, Pony?"

"I should jolly well think so!" declared Pony. "I didn't think she had it in her to make such a priceless fool of herself."

"You've let her get too cocky for words about her voice," said Milly.

"Oh, but she looked so f—f—funny!" giggled Merle.

Helen looked up from the boot-hole in which she was rummaging. "Nice kind of friends *you* are!" she observed quietly. "Kicking a fellow when she's down! I can't tell one note of music from another, but personally I liked it very much."

"So did I!" burst out Sheila from behind Milly. "It was a more difficult song than Milly's. I don't know who let her try to sing such a difficult song, but whoever did it, it wasn't fair. And one day you'll all be laughing on the other side of your faces, so there! You just wait and see!"

Kit came through the cloakroom quietly. "I couldn't help overhearing," she said. "Thank you, Helen."

She caught Pony's eye. Not so very long ago, Pony had been down on her luck, too. But one did not remind people of that. One did not even have to look as if one remembered.

"Thank you, Sheila," she said, and went out into the corridor. She did not look where she was going. She bumped into Miss Binns and nearly upset her cup of tea. Miss Binns put a hand on her arm to steady herself and looked up into her face. Kit was taller than "Fido" now.

"Never mind, dear," she said. "You have only slopped a little of it into the saucer. And I think I am going to get myself another cup, in any case. I want you to have this one. Will you go up into my room and drink it there? You can stay as long as you like. I am going to ask Miss Priestley if you may be excused preparation. I think you have a little headache, dear."

"Thanks awfully, Miss Binns," mumbled Kit, and fled to the staff studies. Nobody saw her go. Miss Binns kept her secret. Rubbing out is a painful process, but when it is all over, one can begin again. When she peeped round the door an hour later, Kit was fast asleep.

17. *"And at Night she will return"*

IT WOULD HAVE been very difficult to explain things to Papa Andreas if he had not already known. As it was, he smiled when she came in, and said: "Terry has told me all about it. So now you had better sing to me."

"I haven't brought anything to sing," she explained awkwardly. "I didn't know whether I had to or not. And I haven't sung a note since that beastly concert. Only I promised Terry I'd come."

"Suppose we begin with *Voi che sapete?*" he suggested amiably.

"Oh *no—*Papa—*please*! Anyhow, I haven't brought it!"

"It's a remarkable thing," smiled Papa Andreas, "but I happen to possess a copy of *Figaro* myself."

He pulled it out from his shelf of Mozart scores and spread it on the music rest. "I have no accompanist this afternoon," he explained. "I thought we might want to have a little talk later."

"That's just what I want!" urged Kit, blushing. "I don't need to sing—least of all *Voi che sapete*. Please, Papa. I know it's too difficult for me. I've learnt my lesson. Don't rub it in."

"Listen, Janey"—she was always to be "Janey" to him—

"Terry tells me that some silly fool of a woman has done you harm. How can I take away that harm if you will not show me what it is?"

He did not argue any more, but began the introduction. She obeyed without further hesitation. She sang it exactly as she had been taught, including the B flat. When she had finished, he snapped down the music rest and leaned his elbows on it.

"You are a brave girl, my Janey," he said. "Now, I will tell you a few things before we begin. First, you must never alter a note of Mozart. You know that? Good. Then, Mozart is one of the most difficult composers to sing. You know that, too? Good. Why? Because he looks so easy. And because he is so simple. It takes greatness to achieve simplicity. And we must work hard before we can achieve greatness. So far, so good. Then, we must never spoil the words to suit the music. Otherwise, we sing nonsense. If a vowel is difficult for us, then we must master that vowel. It may take years to do that. Do you understand, my Janey?"

"Yes," she replied.

"Very well, then, we will start. First, we will take some very deep breaths."

It was surprising how rested she felt. Perhaps the breathing had refreshed her. And the singing was so easy—single notes, then three notes up and down, then five notes up and down, all within a very small compass, very softly, and all on "ah." He did not ask her to sing any high notes at all.

"Next time you come, you will not get off so lightly, my Janey," he said.

"Do you want me to come again?" she asked.

He hesitated for a moment, frowning to himself. "How old are you, Janey?" he asked.

"I shall be sixteen in June," she replied.

"And what are you doing at school?"

"I take School Certificate this summer. I only hope I get through."

"You must get through, Janey. You must forget all about this, and think only of the examination ahead of you. Then you will pass. What do you do next?"

"A great many of the girls stay on another two years for the Higher Certificate. That's what Milly and Helen are working for now. But it all depends on what you're going to take up afterwards."

"What are you going to take up, Janey?"

"I—don't—know. Laura says I must specialize in History for a year, and then take a secretarial course, so that I can be Father's secretary afterwards. He's going to write a book on the Later Minoan Period. Laura says he knows more about it than anybody else in the world."

"And you—would like to do that?"

"No, Papa. I don't know why. I don't know what I want to do."

"You will never know until you are honest with yourself, my Janey. But now you will not worry any more. You will take your School Certificate, and you will not fail. And you will not sing a note. Remember!"

"What about Class Singing, Papa?"

"With that woman?—not for the world! Miss Laura will not mind asking for you to give up Class Singing, will she?"

"Not a bit. She thinks it's a waste of time."

"Very well. That is settled. And some day you will tell me what is in your mind. But not yet, my Janey. Not yet!"

Miles and Terry met her and took her to Waterloo for

the Manningleigh train. They had been friendly ever since they had met in Heryot. Kit sometimes wondered why; they were so very different.

When she reached Belceaster House, she found her great-aunts all in a twitter. "Thy brother Richard is coming to see us tomorrow," Aunt Priscilla told her. "He says he has some news for us, and for thee as well. What dost thou think it can be? Surely they cannot have made him a Professor! He is so very young. But he is certainly a most remarkable young man. I cannot tell how he can do it."

When Kit saw Richard's little sports car drive into the Place, she could hardly believe her eyes. There was a girl with him.

They jumped out and Kit ran down to open the door. For a moment she stood on the threshold, open-mouthed. There was something so familiar about the girl. She had a mop of fair curls and an elfin face. "Flip!" cried Kit. "Why, it's Flip!"

"Of course it is!" laughed Flip, and, greatly to her astonishment, kissed her.

"However did you come to know Flip, Richard?" asked Kit.

"Seeing she has been at Oxford for nearly three years, it hasn't been difficult," laughed Richard. "You ought to be pleased with me for following your example!"

"Of course I am! There's nobody like Flip."

"I thought there wasn't. That's why I'm going one further than you could."

"What *do* you mean, Richard?"

"Kit, you little goose!" laughed Flip. "Can't you understand that I'm going to be your sister?"

It was the best news in the world. When Kit went back

to school, all the girls who had known Flip were wild with
envy. "And your eldest brother is so handsome, too," sighed
Merle. "They'll make a lovely pair."

"Will the wedding be in Chesterham?" asked Pony
eagerly.

"Of course not," replied Kit. "You have to be married in
the place where the bride lives. Flip comes from Middlehampton. So does Miss Priestley, by the way. Do you think
she'll buy a new hat for the wedding?"

"Are you going to be a bridesmaid, Kit?" asked Bendie.
There was a little sneer in her voice.

"You may be sure I am," grinned Kit. "Shan't I spoil the
picture for them? Let's hope they'll ask Milly, too, to make
up for it!"

She did not mind how much they teased her now. That
horrible concert had seemed the very worst thing that could
happen to her. But from the moment she woke up in Fido's
study, she had known that that kind of thing did not matter
any more. She had begun again.

She had very little trouble with School Certificate. She
was glad the results were out before Richard's wedding in
the great Friends' Meeting House at Middlehampton. It was
so much easier to meet Miss Priestley after the suspense was
over, when she knew that she had done well.

The wedding was at the close of the summer holidays.
Flip looked very lovely in her ivory satin gown. Richard's
face lit up as he saw her come into the Meeting House on
her father's arm. She carried a great sheaf of yellow roses.
Kit and Milly walked behind her, dressed alike in misty blue,
with bunches of many-colored sweet-peas. Everybody stood
up as the bride came in; it seemed like a gesture of love from
the throng of relatives and friends who filled the Meeting

House. Tom was there, very serious with his duties as best man; he was so terrified of losing the ring that Charlie accused him of having swallowed it to keep it safe. Miles was looking very handsome, with a red rose in his buttonhole; he had insisted on bringing Terry with him—"It's time he began to get into practice!" he assured Kit gravely, and Kit could not make out what he meant. The dear old aunts from Manningleigh were sitting in front with Great-aunt Susan Spurrier, who was turned ninety now. Kit, meeting her for the first time, looked for the loveliness of which she had heard so much, and found the beauty of holiness in her face. Cousin Charles and Cousin Brenda were there, and Philip and Sheila; as they all sat down again, Kit could see by the look in Sheila's eyes that she was in the thick of one of her romances.

The Professor sat next to Richard, his hand resting on his son's arm. Laura watched anxiously beside him. She was happy about Richard's marriage, of course, and she liked Sylvia, though she considered her rather young, but really nothing mattered beside the welfare of her beloved uncle. Only she did wish Kit would look a bit more on the alert, she was obviously in one of her dreamy moods, and soon it would be time for her to take over the bouquet when Sylvia stood up with Richard. Of course, Milly ought to have been chief bridesmaid. She had told Sylvia so in the beginning, but Sylvia had insisted on having her own way. Perhaps, later on, Sylvia would realize that Laura really knew best.

There was an intense stillness in the Meeting House. Everybody seemed to be waiting for something. That was how a meeting for worship should begin, thought Kit. Her mind flew back to Chesterham Meeting House, and that Sunday morning years ago when she had thought she was so sure of herself: it had all come right in the end, but she knew now that you had to wait for the things that really mattered. Sometimes you had to wait a long time, and sometimes there would be a great loneliness on the top of the wall, but in the end "way would open," as the old Friends used to say. Kit felt strangely at peace. Suddenly she knew that something was going to happen; she turned to Flip with a smile and took the flowers from her as the young couple rose to their feet.

"Thank goodness," thought Laura. "She was only just in the nick of time!"

"How like the dear child," said Aunt Maria to Aunt Priscilla afterwards. "She knew when the right moment came."

Cousin Brenda was suddenly reminded of the Angel Trio. Kit had begun to wake up then, she thought. And now she was losing her old self-consciousness and becoming really sure of herself. There would be changes ahead for a good many people when Kit was finally awake. Cousin Brenda glanced across at Laura, but she was watching the bride and bridegroom so intently that she did not notice her. They were standing in silence, holding each other by the right hand. Laura thought they had forgotten what they had to say, and wondered whether she ought to prompt them.

"In the fear of the Lord and in the presence of this assembly, I take this my friend, Sylvia Felpham, to be my wife," said Richard, speaking strongly and clearly. Sylvia followed him in her soft musical voice. They repeated the beautiful old Quaker promises as if they were the happiest people in the world. Kit thought they probably were. Afterwards, the silence settled down again. Miss Priestley spoke a few words about the Mercy window in Heryot Cathedral, and how that one act of kindness to a former enemy had lived on and flowered through the centuries. She spoke of the influence of dedicated lives, and how none can measure it, because goodness grows. Cousin Charles reminded them all of the adventure of married life, and how all experience, whether of joy or sorrow, should enrich it and beautify it. "Even 'the clouds are big with mercy,'" he said, quoting from Cowper, "but they can't break in blessings on our heads if we walk about with our umbrellas up!" Kit caught Philip's eye. They both had a brief mental picture of Richard and Flip setting up house under an umbrella. But they wouldn't, of course; they weren't afraid of anything so long as they were together. Finally Great-aunt Susan Spurrier knelt down and prayed for God's blessing to rest on the young couple, and all who were standing in the quiet room felt that they had shared in the blessing, too.

After the reception, Miss Priestley asked the Professor and Laura and Kit if they would come to tea next day. The Professor had already been invited to the university, but Laura said that she and Kit would be glad to come. They had a long talk with Miss Priestley, and Laura explained how useful it would be for Kit to be her father's secretary. "He needs somebody more and more," she said. "And of course eventually Kit will want to take over the housekeeping as well. Uncle won't need me at all then."

"It all sounds most interesting, Laura dear," observed Miss Priestley, and blinked mildly.

"She had better specialize in History this year," declared Laura. "What else could she take? She couldn't start short-hand, I suppose?"

"German would be useful," remarked Miss Priestley.

Laura looked mystified. "Why German?" she asked.

"A great many learned books are written in German," said Miss Priestley, blinking faster than ever. "Kit might have to read them. And there is an Italian scholar working on the Mycenaean sites just now. I think she had better begin Italian."

"Of course you know best, Miss Priestley," said Laura. She never could get over the feeling that Miss Priestley was her Headmistress. She felt as if she was back at school again.

"It is so much easier to learn the grammar at school," continued Miss Priestley. "If she keeps up her French and German, and gets a good grounding in Italian, she will make an excellent secretary."

"She had better drop her music," said Laura.

"Do you really think so?" asked Miss Priestley. "Class Singing, I agree. But she is getting on very well now with Miss Fishwick. It would be nice if she could play to her father in the evenings sometimes. Altogether, I think you have arranged it all very nicely, Laura dear. Don't you think so, Kit?"

"Yes, thank you, Miss Priestley," replied Kit. She felt as if the wind had been taken out of her sails. So did Laura.

Altogether, it was a very satisfactory last year at school. Kit was a little sorry that Laura would not consider letting her stay on the extra year for Higher Certificate, but of course it did seem rather an unnecessary expense. Pony and Helen and Milly would all be leaving, too, and she did not really want to stay on when they had gone. Helen was the Head Girl, and Pony was "sub." If only Pony had been in the Upper Sixth, the positions would probably have been reversed. That was something she had lost through her own fault, and she knew it. No head girl at Heryot had ever had a more loyal "sub."

Helen was working hard for a scholarship. She wanted to go to the London School of Economics, but her mother disliked the idea intensely. She said they would turn her into a regular frump. Pony was going to take up medicine. Milly had not decided yet, but she thought she might like to go on the stage. She was growing prettier than ever. All the girls were raving about her singing. Tatty lent her songs, and played for her at the school concerts.

Kit kept her promise loyally; she never sang a note. She had not thought that she would want so badly to sing. She told Terry about it one day at the Chauntesingers, when he was home for the week-end. He told her to practice playing song accompaniments whenever she felt like it. "Play them over and over again, and *think* the line of the song," he explained. "That's how we do part of our practicing. Then try whispering the words to yourself, and speak them as clearly as ever you can, taking the breaths in the right places. And then try to feel what the song is about." He lent her some songs, and told her to ask Old Fish for some more. "You ought to tell her about Papa Andreas. She'll understand!" he said.

"Why don't you come and sing to us at school sometimes, Terry?" she asked.

Terry grinned. "I'm not putting my head into a hornet's nest of chattering schoolgirls, even for you," he said. "It's all right for Simon Trent—he doesn't live near the place! But don't you worry, Kit. Some day I'll sing there with you."

She laughed and carried the songs back to school with her. Then she took her courage in both hands and explained the situation to Old Fish. She had not expected her to be so sympathetic. She worked out the phrasing with her and showed her how to take the breaths. "You would have time for a big one here," she pointed out. "But there you would have to take a catch-breath through the vowel."

"What do you mean?" asked Kit.

"You mustn't let the audience see you breathe," she explained. "Not but what some singers gasp like fishes! But that's neither here nor there. The last word in that phrase is 'you'; you would keep your lips rounded for the 'oo' sounds, and breathe through it. See?"

"Why couldn't I breathe through my nose?" asked Kit.

"Try it!" smiled Miss Fishwick.

"I suppose it wouldn't work. Still, I ought to be good at sniffing, you know. My great-grandfather used to blow out the candles with his nose!"

It was more fun than she had ever thought it could be. She told nobody about it, until Pony found out by accident during their last term. Pony was unexpectedly understanding. "I've always felt rotten about that day after the concert," she confessed. "We were all pigs to you, except Helen and Sheila. I was the worst of the lot. Yes, I was! I ought to have stuck up for you. When Helen flashed out at us, I felt a worm. And afterwards, I never said I was sorry. I couldn't. You were so different."

"I was," said Kit. "But that's all over now, Pony. I didn't tell you about this because—well, it's a sort of secret. Bendie and Merle and the rest of them would snigger if they knew, but it isn't only that. Tatty would laugh at Old Fish."

"Kit!" said Pony suddenly. "I want you to do something for me."

"What on earth?"

"I want you to sing at the Leavers' Concert."

"I can't, Pony. I've promised Papa Andreas. Besides, you've got Milly."

"I know. She'll sing, of course. But she's always the same, you know. I want you, too. You could write to Mr. What's-his-name, couldn't you? Or Old Fish could?"

Kit hesitated.

"Please," urged Pony.

Just then Old Fish came in. Kit thought that would settle it. It did, but not in the way she had expected. Old Fish said that she would write herself.

It was to be a bigger Leavers' Concert than usual. Some Old Girls had been selected as members of a team of medical relief workers to be flown out to a district in India which had been devastated by an earthquake. Miss Priestley had decided that this would be a good opportunity for an appeal to be made in aid of their work. There were some talented girls among the Leavers, so that the concert was sure to be an especially good one, parents and friends were to be invited and, as one of the Old Girls concerned was the daughter of the Sheriff, some of the civic dignitaries were coming, too. Milly was going to sing Purcell's "Nymphs and Shepherds"; she was to play the fiddle as well, and would obviously be the star of the concert. Tatty was going to accompany her. "You don't expect me to play for Kit Haverard, do you, darling?" she asked Pony, who was in charge of the arrangements. "Because I really couldn't. Once is enough!"

"You needn't worry. Miss Fishwick will do it!" said Pony shortly. She was beginning to feel, like some of the other girls, that the gilt was a little tarnished on Tatty's gingerbread.

At first Kit could not decide what to sing. She was desperately nervous. Miss Fishwick would not let her sing out much. She made her do deep-breathing exercises every day. Then she would let her do three notes up and down, very softly, on "ah," three notes, and then five. She only let her use the middle part of her voice.

"Papa Andreas's pupils have to stick to this kind of thing for months," she said. "They add the other vowel sounds little by little, as they learn the right shapes for them. I mustn't bother you with all that now, or you'll get muddled. You want to forget all about it on the night and think about the song."

Kit suddenly decided to sing an Irish cradle song. It was one which she had found among Terry's oddments, and at first Old Fish tried to persuade her to change her mind. But somehow it haunted Kit. She could not think of anything else. Old Fish saw that it was no use worrying her any more.

She had the last place on the program. It was usually the place of honor. "You can't put me there!" she cried to Pony in dismay. "Think what a come-down I'll be after Milly."

"I don't care," said Pony. "That's my look-out."

Kit sat miserably at the back of the audience, all through the concert. She did wish her hands would not shake so. Her heart thumped so violently that it almost made her feel sick. Milly sang as prettily as ever, but it was her violin solo which brought down the house. The girls had grown a little tired of Milly's singing; it always seemed to be the same.

Walking on to the stage presented no difficulties this time. Old Fish had shown Kit how to practice it. Still, she could not restrain a little gasp when she saw Papa Andreas sitting with Terry among the Chauntesingers. She looked round at Old Fish, and Old Fish whispered "Ready?" in a quiet, steady voice. She pulled herself together and nodded. The introduction began softly and slowly.

She had not realized that singing was so like her old

pretending-games.

> *O men from the fields*
> *Come softly within,*
> *Tread softly, softly,*
> *O men coming in.*

They were tramping across the earthen floor, a slow procession of men with bowed heads and shabby working clothes. Their great hands swung as they walked. And they must tread softly, softly.

> *For mavourneen's goin'*
> *From me and from you,*
> *Where Mary will fold him*
> *With mantle of blue.*

The rain was streaming down outside the cottage, and the wind was howling. Oh, to be safe in the cloudy blue mantle when the things were prowling outside!

> *From reek of the smoke,*
> *And cold of the floor,*
> *And peering of things*
> *Across the half-door.*

There they were—horrible! horrible! She could see them in the half-light, leering, gibbering across at her, and stretching out crooked fingers to drag the child away. But they could not do it. She knew they couldn't. They had no power to harm anybody really. They could not touch the "Light Within."

O men from the fields,
Soft, softly come through,
Mary puts round him
Her mantle of blue.

The accompaniment died away into the stillness. There was not a sound in the great hall. Kit stood motionless on the platform. She was still looking at the mantle of blue.

Then suddenly the applause broke out. Kit started and looked round at Old Fish. Then she bowed shyly and walked off the platform.

"Encore! Encore!" shouted the girls, and the contingent of brothers from Marston stamped rhythmically with their feet. The rows of friends and parents clapped and exclaimed alternately. At last Old Fish brought Kit on again. It was some time before the applause died down sufficiently for her to be heard.

She sang the little folk-song which she had sung to the Chauntesingers: "As I was a-walking." She could almost smell the hawthorn on the bushes. The ploughboy was whistling in the distance, and the larks were rising up into the blue sky. Up and up they flew until their songs were lost in the sunshine. Yet their own nests on Mother Earth would draw them home again.

The applause thundered out, and the visitors clapped and cheered. Old Fish struck up the School Hymn. It was time the girls were in bed.

Kit came down the corridor, her eyes shining. She met Miss Priestley and Papa Andreas as they came out of the hall together.

"Well?" smiled Papa Andreas, as he took her hand. "Now

can you tell me what is in your mind?"

"And now do you know what you want to do?" asked Miss Priestley.

"Yes," answered Kit with her head held high. "Yes, I know now. I'm going to sing!" She looked very like Janey. Her eyes were full of tears.

Sir Geoffrey Chauntesinger came up and shook her by the hand. "You dratted little Quaker!" he growled. "So you've done it again, hey?"

Terry said nothing. He did not need to.

Miss Binns popped out from behind Miss Priestley and laid her hand lightly on Kit's arm. "I want you to come up to my room now, dear," she said. "I'm going to make you a nice hot cup of tea."

Songs Referred To

The Lark in the Morn is one of the Somersetshire folksongs collected and arranged by Cecil J. Sharp and published by Messrs. Novello & Co., Ltd. *O Men from the Fields* is a poem by Padraic Colum, set to music by Herbert Hughes and published by Messrs. Boosey & Co., Ltd.

Chapter 7:
> *So wahr die Sonne scheinet (So Truly the Sun Seems)*,
> Schumann

Chapter 10:
> *An die Leier (To the Street Organ)*, Schubert
> *Die Liebe hat gelogen (Love Has Lied)*, Schubert
> *Nacht und Traume (Night and Dreams)*, Schubert
> *Die Forelle (The Trout)*, Schubert
> *Gruppe aus dem Tartarus (Group from Tartarus)*,
> Schubert
> *Wohin (Wherein?)*, Schubert
> *Der Musensohn (The Son of the Muses)*, Schubert
> *Erlkonig (The Earl King)*, Schubert
> *An die Musik (To Music)*, Schubert
>> *Du holde Kunst, in wieviel grauen Stunden*
>> *(Thou beloved art, in how many gray hours)*
>> *Du holde Kunst, ich danke dir (Thou beloved*
>> *art, I thank thee)*

Chapter 16:
> *Voi che sapete (You who know)*, from *The Marriage of Figaro*, Mozart

About the Author

Elfrida Vipont Brown was born in Manchester, England in 1902, into an active Quaker heritage. She attended schools in Manchester and York, not unlike "Chesterham High School" and "Heryot School" in *The Lark in the Morn*. After a time reading history at Manchester University, she realized that what she really wanted to do was to sing, and she went on to study singing with teachers in London, Paris and Leipzig. In 1926 she married R.P. Foulds, a research technologist.

During World War II she was headmistress of an Evacuation School set up by Quakers in Manchester and Liverpool at Yealand Conyers, a small village in Lancashire,where children from those cities and from farther afield were sent for safety, away from the wartime bombing raids.Three of her own four daughters were pupils at this school.

Elfrida Foulds had already published three books for children before the war, and after it was over she became a writer in many fields, with interests (reflected in her "Lark" books) in history, Quakerism and music. She wrote nearly two dozen novels, stories and anthologies for children and young adults. *The Lark in the Morn* and *The Lark on the Wing* are among the best of many fine books. *The Lark on the Wing* won the Carnegie Medal in 1951.

Writing under the names of Elfrida Vipont and Charles Vipont, Mrs Foulds lived for many years at Yealand Conyers, while traveling worldwide for Quaker committees and lecturing in schools and libraries. She died in 1992.